FATE'S MISTRESS

Book Three of The Three Graces Trilogy

LAURA DU PRE

ESCAPE TO THE COURT

Join Laura's mailing list and receive a complementary copy of the sequel, *Safe in My Arms*.

ABOUT FATE'S MISTRESS

Travel back to the court of the French Renaissance

Fate's Mistress: Book Three of the Three Graces Trilogy

Fate can be a cruel mistress...

Cousins to the King of Navarre, the Cleves sisters witness the glamour and danger of the French royal court firsthand. Middle sister, Catherine, is married to the Duc de Guise, the most rabid Catholic in France. Ambitious and well-connected, Guise is the main rival for the French throne, which is currently occupied by an unpopular Henri III.

Guise managed to win concessions from Henri, but concessions come with a steep price on his head. As his Duchesse, Catherine is in a dangerous position of her own. Determined to play her part in bringing about the downfall of the Valois and the rise of the Guise, Catherine will risk her own safety.

But is the risk worth the rewards? Will either of them escape with their lives? Catherine has to take a chance for herself, and the consequences will change French history.

Based on a true story

The Cleves sisters' story concludes with Catherine, who stands in the middle of court politics in France of the 1500s. Like most great noble families of the period, the web of intermarriages and alliances made enemies out of blood relatives. It also meant that the stories of the people who served the Valois monarchs were as intertwined and as complicated as their marriages.

Led by the ever-vigilant Catherine de Medici, Queen Mother of France and a force of nature, the members of the court shaped the political and religious future of France of the Sixteenth Century. In the trilogy, you'll meet the often- derided Charlotte, Madame de Sauve, and enough royal mistresses to satisfy your need for scandal.

❦ I ❦

H otel de Guise, November 1586

"HENRI, FOR GOD'S SAKE—SLOW DOWN! I CANNOT KEEP UP. MY legs are too short!" I watched as my husband's wide shoulders trailed down the hallway before me, his enraged voice booming from the thick, stone walls. I scurried behind him, doing my best to keep pace with him. When he was in one of his rages, there was no reasoning with him. Yet, that fact had never stopped me before. I was in the third month of my latest pregnancy, my twelfth, and could still scamper behind my husband.

His hulking legs continued to put him further away from me, taking one step to match my two. I was far from the shortest woman at court, but Henri, the Duc de Guise, was a giant of a man. No man in France could measure up to his height, the blond giant towered over every man at court. Unfortunately for me, he had a personality to match his oversized body.

"Henri!" I screeched at the top of my lungs, taking my turn in the game we had perfected in the two decades of our marriage. Neither of us would fit a priest's view of a Godly or virtuous man or woman, but then, neither of us had attempted to pretend that we were anything other than what we were. This arrangement made it easy to be honest with one another. Our determination to be brutally honest with one another that we found ourselves in screaming matches with one another, but on this one occasion, I was not the person who had enraged my hulking husband.

The person in question was his August Majesty, King Henri III of France, Duc d' Anjou and only surviving son of Catherine de Medici. Last summer, my husband and his Catholic League had successfully compelled the king to agree to place him in charge of the armies of France. My husband immediately appointed his younger brother, the Duc de Mayenne to attack the Protestants that swarmed across France. When the terms were set in the heat of summer, we breathed a sigh of relief that the king had finally come to his senses and protected France from invasion and the threat of heresy from the Protestant queen of England and my heretic cousin, the King of Navarre.

Today, however, my husband received word from his spies in Normandy that the king had spent the last three months in secret negotiations with the Protestants behind his back. All the work that Mayenne did on the battlefield was for nothing. Worse still the king casually broke his promise to the Guise brothers to follow their advice in leading the armies of France.

I continued to catch up with him, but he stormed out of the front door of our house and onto the courtyard below, where a saddled horse always waited for him. Watching him so, I seethed. I knew where he was going. He would see that strumpet.

Do not misunderstand me—I am no moralist who chafes at a philandering husband. I have had my share of lovers myself. I am too lively to be satisfied with a single man, even if that man is my husband; even if he is arguably the most handsome man at court. I have never begrudged Henri for his mistresses as he has rarely objected to my lovers. I object to the idea that he is going to take out his frustration with another woman, while ignoring me. I have spent too many years in service to the Guise family to allow them to shut me out today.

I storm back to my own rooms, passing one of the many retainers who have sworn loyalty to the Guise and the Catholic League. Our cavernous home, the Hotel de Guise, purchased by the previous Duke and my mother-in-law, has more than enough room to house the people necessary to sustain a rebellion. Every person in this house has been a party to the seditious acts against the king and his favorites. As one of my husband's most ardent allies, I do not take well to being shut out of his council.

Once at my desk, I pulled out a pen and paper and composed letters to allies across France. My husband might not want to acknowledge my usefulness to the League, but there were many people who would. After he finished having his sport in bed, we would have words.

❧

"Every time I think Henri Valois cannot sink any further, he surprises me!" My sister-in-law, the widowed Duchesse de Montpensier, sat her wine on the table before her, careful not to spill any on the intricate lace cloth before her. Her wording was deliberate; while the rest of us still continued to refer to the man on the throne of France as the King, she insisted on insulting him by referring to him as "Henri Valois" as if he were an ordinary citizen. If Montpensier had her way, he would soon become an ordinary citizen. Amongst the noblewomen who ran the female contingent of the League, she was the most ardent. There was no moderation in her tone or in her actions. If she ran the League, Catherine of Lorraine would gladly march upon the Louvre and burn the King in his bed as he slept.

"You would think for his own survival, he would take advice from someone other than that useless fop Épernon." As soon as the man's name was out of my mouth, I ground my teeth. Épernon enjoyed the place that rightfully belonged to my husband and the members of the Guise and Lorraine families. As the highest-ranking nobles of France, their place was at the king's hand. Yet, Henri III had raised up virtual peasants to the lucrative posts that kept the nobles from going into virtual bankruptcy. It had forced far too many of our retainers and allies to sell land and assets to make up for losing offices that were rightfully theirs.

"If he had common sense." She absentmindedly picked at the ruffs at her wrists. "He would listen more to your brother-in-law." I groaned inwardly at her accusation. My brother-in-law was the man who had risen with the king's ascension to the throne; and a man who had long-served the Valois kings of France. Louis Gonzaga, who took over my father's title of Duc de Nevers by marrying my older sister, was the only voice of reason left in the king's privy chamber. Louis' continued presence there gave us hope that eventually, he would get through to the king. Yet, judging by the king's past decisions, he would ignore Louis as soon as Épernon whispered into his royal ear.

I shook my head, "I never know what is in Louis' mind. I know that part of him agrees passionately with the League. He is as loyal a Catholic as we are. Yet, he works to remain as neutral as he can. It's as if he's terrified to stand up and decide."

She shrugged, "Then speak to Henriette. She is your sister." *I can no more control my sister than my husband can control his*, I thought, as I avoided Montpensier's gaze. As controlling as the woman who sat before me was, Henriette was just as nebulous. I never knew her mind either. Sometimes, I felt as if my sister was a cold, calculating fish.

"I have a relationship with my sister, and the king himself made it so." Henriette was once the most senior woman in the queen's house-hold, as well-placed in the king's court as her husband. In a characteristically stupid move, however, the king decided one evening to trap my sister in a fake affair and "expose" Henriette before the court. She fled from the court in humiliation and has barely made any effort to return. If I wish to see her, I usually have to drop by the Hotel de Nevers and make a sisterly visit. Even though it is selfish, I am very put out by her self-imposed exile from court. Without her, I have few real friends to rely upon, save my radical sister-in-law. Montpensier is quite a handful, angrily railing against the king at every opportunity. I count myself as a radical, but her extremism gets on my nerves regularly.

"Catherine, you mentioned the new printing blocks—would you show them to me?"

She clapped her hands. "Of course! I was afraid you would never ask. Come!" Standing, she pulled me up from my chair and dragged me outside as I struggled to put on my heavy cape. The damp cold settled on Paris this time of the year, bringing with it a heavy fog over the river. With an almost gleeful bounce in her step, she led me to the stables of her Hotel de Guise and at an empty stall, she glanced both ways and opened the padlock.

"Here they are. The carvers finished just last week. I paid them well for their silence." Throwing back a horse blanket, she showed the wooden printing blocks. One of them depicted the King of France as a priest, shorn of his hair and shorn of his crown. "The price of betrayal of Gaul." the inscription screamed in bold lettering. Another featured a Protestant army, marching upon the familiar walls of Paris, with babies hanging aloft on pikes. I glanced at Montpensier, "Isn't that a trifle much?" My stomach lurched at the sight and the wave of nausea caused by my pregnancy.

"Innocents suffer in war, and if the Protestants and their mercenaries from Germany and Switzerland march across France without opposition, there is no telling what horrors the city will endure. It is best we acknowledge the danger and do something before this image comes true!" Her eyes shone with the passion of a fanatic. In those brown depths, I saw a touch of madness. Still, I knew that I had few friends and allies in Paris, and given how Henri had pushed me away a few days before, I could not afford to alienate his sister. Instead, I turned to look at another plate.

"This one doesn't have an image," I frowned, trying to make sense. She made a reverse nod, acknowledging my confusion.

"This is blank so we can create pamphlets from it. The lines are there to make the sentences straight. Here," she rummaged around in the hay until she found a small sack, "are the individual letters that the printers will use to make the pamphlets. The beauty of this is that we can use many combinations of letters. We can make several pamphlets and we can do it."

"And are you certain you want them taken from your house? At least there, you can have complete control over the printing process." Something told me that the wooden blocks in front of me were a portent of trouble, but I did not know just how troublesome they would later prove to be. For the moment, my main objection was the added activity they would bring to my home.

She shrugged, "Henri promised. As I am a widow, it would not do for someone to see me instigating rebellion against the king's policies." My mouth snapped open in shock. Was she serious? There was no woman in Paris better known for instigating and fermenting rebellion against the king! Why would she bother to stop now? Had she finally realized that she had gone too far? Did she know that the blocks were too dangerous? Yes, her sex would cause the king to have mercy on her if someone found the blocks at her home, but it was not a given. She faced just as much danger as the rest of us.

Still, I wanted to show my usefulness to my husband. Having control of the words printed by the League across the city of Paris carried with it an irresistible amount of power. Despite my earlier sense of foreboding, I turned to her.

"I'll see that Philobert finds a place for him at the Hotel de Guise." At least inside my home, they would be under my control. I would see to that.

❦

LIFE AT THE COURT WAS TAXING FOR ME. SINCE 1579, MY HUSBAND and the king openly quarreled, and the king constantly took pains to make little insults towards my husband and every member of his family. Once the two were playmates, a reflection of the vaunted position that the Guise and my mother-in-law, a granddaughter of a king, enjoyed at court. Soon after the king came to the throne, however, he allowed other men to poison his once close friendship with my husband.

Never at a loss for ambitious men to fawn over him, the king had selected a man named Quelus and another, Charles de Balsac, Sieur d'Entragues. as his particular favorites in the fashionable sport of dueling. This dueling was not a method of satisfying honor, more play-acting to amuse the king and his close friends. Having the king's favor made a man reckless, none more so than Quelus. The men were stupid enough to engage in a duel, killing both of them. The king mourned Quelus so much that the city came out in droves to mock him. Entragues sought and received sanctuary at the Hotel de Guise.

Thinking he was doing his old friend a favor, my husband readily tended to the king's favorite, working in vain to keep the man alive, despite his injuries. To our horror, the king turned on both d'Entragues and my husband.

Demanding the body of d'Entragues, the king raged against my husband, accusing him of rebellion against him. When my flabbergasted husband replied that he was doing the King's will, the King went to even more extremes. He stated that d'Entragues came to our home because he was carrying on an affair with me and he sought my aid. I have never been faithful to my husband, but even I would never be desperate enough to lie with one of those effeminate favorites. I would sooner lie with a peasant from the fields of Navarre. My husband did not fall for the ruse and buried the man without releasing his body to the king. From that point on, we became a continuous target for the king's ire.

As if this ongoing unpleasantness were not enough, there are enough base individuals at court to make me question the standards of the court. At the forefront of these individuals, is the woman I know to be my husband's current mistress.

Charlotte de Beaune-Semblancy is nothing more than the descendent of a silversmith and the great-granddaughter of a known traitor. By her first marriage, she became Baroness de Sauve. By her second marriage, she had finally ascended to the nobility to become the Marquise de Noirmoutier. She is coarse and with no breeding at all. Every time I am forced to see her, I feel the bile rising in my mouth.

It is easy to blame my hatred of the woman on her common origins. Yet, I have many more reasons to hate her. She is the Queen Mother's creature, one of her Flying Squadron who spends their days and evenings in various men's beds, coyly plying information from them at the Queen Mother's behest. While most women at court choose their bedfellows for passion or for sport, these women do it for money. Charlotte is one of Catherine de Medici's most accomplished whores, managing the feat of juggling two lovers at once. Even in France, that was quite a task. At her mistresses' command, she jumped between the beds of my cousin, the King of Navarre, and the king's younger brother and heir, until she had alienated the men to a degree they barely trusted one another. I blame her for alienating them from the king's youngest sister and my sister, Henriette's close friend, Queen Margot of Navarre. Thanks to Charlotte's machinations, the king stripped Margot of her allies at court and left with few friends at court, save my sister.

This behavior was despicable enough, but no act is too shameful for that Circe. I hold Charlotte directly responsible for breaking my sister's heart over a decade ago. While Henriette mourned the sudden death of her only son, she found solace in the arms of a lover. Charlotte schemed to find evidence that sent Henriette's lover to his death. My poor sister endured those losses within a month of one another, at the time when I thought she might die as well of heartbreak. For these reasons and more, I have no reservations in admitting my hatred of Charlotte.

As I attended the Queen Mother, I kept a wary eye out for Charlotte. I was in no mood to deal with the snake. "Madame de Guise, please hand me my ruff," the Queen Mother gestured towards me and I moved forward.

"Here, your Majesty." I spread my hands over the foamy folds, doing my best to straighten them so they would sit high around her fleshy neck. The Queen Mother nodded her approval of my efforts and I stepped back from her.

"Someone is missing," I heard a sly voice whisper behind me. It was one of the sharp-tongued Mademoiselles. Most of the women my age and older in the queen's household knew better than to engage in gossip directly in front of her. She publicly decries any hint of scandal, while meeting with her Squadron behind closed doors. It is one of the many hypocrisies that Catherine de Medici has created during her long years at the French court.

"It's Madame de Noirmoutier.! I wonder where she is!" A giggle spilled out from a mouth behind me and I fought the urge to turn around and slap the offender.

"I think it's better to ask where she's been!" This time, the laughter is louder, drawing the queen's annoyance.

"If you girls have anything to say, I suggest you say it out loud so we can all hear. No? Then, I suppose you are gossiping. That is a sin and you are both to go to confession to absolve yourselves of your sin." Catherine directed her words at the two offenders and I felt impressed with her ability to hear. Craning my neck around to witness their humiliation, I saw one girl's mouths snap open. The other girl only blushed furiously. Wordlessly, they both curtsied and made their escape from the Queen Mother's privy chamber.

I AVOIDED CHARLOTTE'S PRESENCE UNTIL THAT AFTERNOON, AS THE ladies of the Queen Mother's retinue sat and played cards. I exhaled loudly, annoyed as she floated into the room and made her reverence to the queen. "Forgive me, Madame. My son is sick, and I was attending to him."

Catherine searched her face as if looking to detect a lie. "I will pray for your son's health. See it does not happen again, Madame de Noirmoutier." The Queen Mother's behavior surprised me; was Charlotte acting independently of her Mistress' instructions?

Like the other ladies of the court, I was smart enough to avoid an open quarrel with Charlotte, which meant that it forced me to be civil to her in the Queen Mother's presence. Away from the sharp eyes of Catherine de Medici, however, the woman was fair game. I would have to bide my time. Spying my mother-in-law across the chamber, I rose and took a seat next to her. She was reading a book in Italian. Like the Queen Mother, she was an Italian, and they often spoke in their native language to ease their homesickness. While I could speak and read Italian, I was far from a native speaker.

"What are you reading?" I gazed over at Anna d' Este, the Dowager Duchesse de Guise and Nemours, who smiled to acknowledge my presence. She gave me a quick motherly squeeze on my forearm.

"Plutarch." Anna was one of the most educated women at court and she had imparted her love of history to her son. While my husband preferred reading the history of warfare, his mother preferred the philosophers. Her taste in reading material made it much easier for me to talk to her.

"How many times have you read it?'"

She shrugged, "Not enough. I get more out of it each time I read it. You look uncomfortable."

I shifted in my chair and tried to sit without pressing against the nerves of my back. I was carrying my twelfth child, proof that my marriage had been a fruitful one. Our children provided the Guise family with plenty of sons and daughters to marry across France. Five of our children lay buried in the family crypt back in Joinville, close to the eastern border of France. Losing a child was a common event, but losing each one was an agony for me. After carrying a being who depended upon me for almost a year and caring for it after its birth, the sudden loss was excruciating. I never got used to the threat of losing a baby, no woman ever did.

Of our healthy children, most lived at the nursery in faraway Lorraine, where my husband's formidable grandmother had raised generations of children. Most noble families in France entrusted their daughters to Antoinette de Bourbon's capable hands. A year ago, the aged Antoinette died, which meant that my youngest, Renee, lived with us at the Hotel de Guise. It thrilled me that my daughter was with me in Paris and hardly missed an opportunity to tend to her myself.

"I understand my daughter is off making mischief again." Her sharp eyes missed nothing. It was not my place to shield Catherine of Lorraine from her own mother; if Anna planned on upbraiding her for her actions, that was her prerogative. Still, I did not want to implicate myself and put myself in an awkward position with my influential mother-in-law.

"She's still dealing with Louis' estate. She's cleaning out his personal items, finally." That was partly true—the elderly Duc de Montpensier had crammed their home with items and now, Catherine faced the overwhelming task of dispensing with them. We packed many items off to the far corners of France to her step-children as part of their inheritance. Others were collecting dust until Catherine could sell them and make a profit. Overall, she was luckier than most of us— her husband had left her quite a fortune and she did not have to handle paying off the taxes from her father's death over a decade ago. That duty fell to his heir, a burden Henri faced when his father died suddenly in 1563.

"I doubt that everything in that house qualifies as a priceless antique. Some of those items might bring another kind of price, no?" She continued to scan my face, and I squirmed.

"This child will not get off of my back!" I cried out loudly enough that the entire room could hear me, hoping to change the subject. The matrons in the Queen Mother's entourage gave me tight smiles of sympathy. Anyone who had carried a child before knew the daily discomforts that came with the condition. Beside me, Anna snorted but let the subject drop.

❦   2   ❧

The next morning, I heard a commotion in the courtyard below my chambers. Considering how frequently troops rushed in and out of our home, I barely noted it. After breakfast, however, my husband strode into my chambers. "Catherine, I'm leaving for Normandy."

"Why would you possibly need to go to Normandy?" It was on the tip of my tongue to ask if he would spend time with Charlotte de Sauve, but I stopped myself from saying it. I had no desire to sound like a clinging, jealous wife. That wasn't in my nature.

"My spies in England just reported that Elizabeth plans to send in more English troops to aid the king. Apparently, they've become closer allies than I'd feared." The thought made me nauseous, if the king was cozying up to the English Queen, then he really was planning on allying with the Protestants.

"Are those troops going to fight Spain or Frenchmen?"

Henri sobered, "Frenchmen. I'm going with Mayenne to shore up Eu." Eu was my county, one precariously close to the English coast, in the heart of Normandy. If Henri wanted to build fortified strongholds in Normandy, it could only mean they were there to protect France against English invasion.

"You could be taking a gamble; if those troops coming from England are there to fight the Spanish and you engage them, you are openly committing treason. Your spies might not be as loyal as you think they are. They could set you up for a trap."

He shrugged; for years, he'd been all but committing treason, but since last July, he had control over all French forces. As General of France, he had the right to defend the country, but this could lead to an open declaration of war against the English.

"What does Mendoza say about this latest adventure?" The Spanish ambassador had virtually moved into our home, constantly dictating to my husband what Spain expected him to do with French forces. Henri had long since grown tired of being treated like a puppet of Spain. When he first solicited Spanish help, he needed the money to finance his campaign against the king. We were now financially insolvent thanks to the income from his late grandmother's estate, so his dependence upon Spanish money was not as strong as it once was.

"He says Elizabeth Tudor will slaughter my cousin Mary Stuart and then kill every Catholic in England." *Slaughter every Catholic*, Henri and Montpensier loved to use that apocalyptic threat to scare people into allying with the Catholic League to save the church from its enemies. I'd grown tired of the same threat thrown against anyone who wavered in their support of the League. I had yet to see any slaughter coming from England.

"Your cousin is being reckless and stupid, plotting out in the open against Elizabeth." Mary, Queen of Scots and the daughter of Henri's only aunt was being held under close guard at Elizabeth's pleasure. Anyone could see the danger Mary was in with her claim to Elizabeth's throne and her male heir. Anyone, that is, but Mary. She'd been foolhardy since her youth as France's Dauphine and later, Queen to the king's older brother, Francis II. Once she returned to her own kingdom of Scotland, however, she became a lethal threat to Elizabeth, challenging her for the English throne.

"I've decided to set up a school for the sons of Catholic nobles from England. They're fleeing in terror and someone needs to show them that there are loyal Catholics somewhere in Europe."

That got my attention, "And just where will you put that school?"

"At Eu. If anyone asks, I'm helping refugees from England to get settled in France."

"You plan to set up some kind of spy factory masquerading as a charity home on my territory?" I turned on him, completely at the end of my patience. "I am not about to let you use my inheritance to ferment a rebellion against the crown! If you plan to do so, there are many Guise properties you can use to defy the king!"

He rolled his eyes, "Legally, they are *all* Guise properties."

"Law be damned! I will not allow you to trample all over me!" The insufferable lout had the nerve to turn and walk away from me. I was not about to let him end our conversation like that. "How dare you walk away from me! You will not touch one timber of my chateau; do you hear me? Henri! Henri!" He sped up his pace until he was so far ahead of me I could not keep up. We raced through the halls of the Hotel de Guise until we were outside in the courtyard. Henri raced, while I waddled as much as my expanding body would allow. The assembled crowd turned to watch the spectacle we were making, but I could not have cared less.

"Are you really going to ignore me and ride out of Paris without a word?"

He mounted his horse and turned to face me, his expression droll. "Goodbye, wife." Before I could respond, he turned around and rode out of the courtyard.

LOATH AS I AM TO ADMIT IT, I WAS WRONG. IN THE SPRING OF 1587, as I rocked my newest daughter Jeanne, a messenger appeared at the doorway of the nursery. The letter he carried stated that Elizabeth of England had finally signed the death warrant for Mary Stuart and that they had beheaded her less than a week ago. I never thought Elizabeth would take the drastic step of killing another anointed monarch, no matter how many stupid intrigues Mary carried out under Elizabeth's nose. Mary's death would be a blow to the French, not only had she been Queen of France, she was a Guise. Henri would feel her execution as a direct challenge to his family.

Sighing, I stood and swept the dust from my skirt. Montpensier would soon likely be banging my door down in disgust over Mary's untimely death. No matter how much the empty-headed woman deserved her death, she would soon become a martyr to French Catholics. Before I could make plans to leave to speak to Montpensier and my mother-in-law, a message came from the Louvre. The Queen wished to see me.

Queen Louise was easily the least problematic person of the Royal Family. A member of the House of Lorraine, she was another of my husband's many and well-placed cousins. Unlike Mary Stuart, however, this queen gave no one a moment of grief with her behavior. I had been part of her retinue since the previous July when Henri wrestled command of the armies from the king's favorites. In passive-aggressive spite, the king removed me from serving his aging mother and into the Queen's household. Since Louise had no public presence, the king thought to wall me up in the Queen's rooms where I would do no harm. If the king thought I would feel slighted by the assignment, he was mistaken. Serving Louise took up so little of my time I had plenty of extra moments to aid my husband and his family in promoting the League in Paris. As my mother-in-law continued to serve the Queen Mother, I was always welcome to visit her in her apartments. If anything, the king made my life much easier.

I found Queen Louise in her privy chamber, directing her maids in packing. "Madame de Guise, I'm sure you've heard the horrible news about Queen Mary." She crossed herself as a reflex. For many people, the gesture was a perfunctory move, but for the pious queen, it was an earnest expression of her compassion for a fellow queen.

"Yes, Madame. I have not spoken to my mother-in-law or the Duchesse de Montpensier, but I'm sure they the feel by the news." Hysterical and milking it for all that it was worth might be a better way of putting things. The longer I avoided speaking to Montpensier, the more dramatic she would be by the time we met. We could reason with Anna with since she had actual memories of her shallow and often empty-headed niece.

"I have told the king that I wish to go to Abbey d'Ardenne to pray for the deliverance of Queen Mary's soul." The abbey was an odd choice. Although it was one of the many that counted Louise as its patron, the location was what caught my attention. Located outside of the town of Caen, it was firmly in Normandy. Since storming out of our home several months ago, my husband had worked to secure Normandy as League territory in an affront to the king.

"Madame, are you sure that such a trip would be safe? The English have taken the life of a Catholic queen, and it may put France in jeopardy." Besides, I could not imagine the king allowing his wife to travel to Normandy where rumors swirled her Lorraine and Guise relations were building up an armed resistance. Was the king oblivious to the resistance building up against his rule?

Caen was also temptingly close to my county of Eu and close to my husband. Going there would give me an opportunity to speak with him in person and see what his plans were now that Mary Stuart was no more. At one time, before the birth of her son, James, Mary had named Phillip of Spain as her heir to the Scottish throne. What would Phillip's reaction be to her death? I could learn little in Paris, but in Normandy, I could speak with Henri in person.

"The king feels I would be safe if you accompanied me to the abbey." Although the queen said this with no hint of artifice, I detected behind-the-scenes machinations of the king giving her permission to go. I would accompany her as a warning to the League she was not be kidnapped or held for ransom. I would go as insurance she would return to Paris without the king being forced to ransom for her release. If the League were stupid enough to attack the queen on the way to the abbey, it would smoke out the traitors for all to see. As a result, the League would not dare make any attempt on the queen during this pilgrimage.

I dashed off a quick letter to Anna, telling her of the queen's desire to make a pilgrimage and of the king's hand in ensuring that I would accompany her. Anna was astute enough to know that the king was positioning me as a pawn in this trip to Caen. I planned to take time out during our trip to Abbey d'Ardenne to make the short ride to my chateau at Eu. True to his nature, my husband had defied me and set up a school under the Jesuits for the "poor Catholics driven out by the English heretics". My husband might have thought he had outmaneuvered me by hiding his activities in Normandy, but he hadn't counted on my determination to check on those activities.

⚜

AS I'D PREDICTED, I FOUND MONTPENSIER MOANING THE TRAGIC death of her cousin, Mary Stuart. "That snake Henri Valois just sat there and did nothing! He had it in his power to save her, and he sat by and let her die. If *that* isn't proof he is on the English payroll, I don't know what is. France has to do something about him. This goes far beyond consorting with heretics. Before long, they'll rule us, whether it's Navarre or Elizabeth herself!" Since the king's younger brother died two years earlier, France faced with the prospect of Henry of Navarre being the only heir to the throne which meant inevitably, a Protestant would rule us. The Catholic League found the idea of France ruled by a heretic was an abomination and no one thought that more than Montpensier.

I sometimes wondered if her passion came from a true devotion to her religion or some other reason. She often gave me the feeling she was mentally unbalanced, giving into one fit of hysterics or another. Perhaps, she thrived on melodrama and the thrill of inciting rebellion. Whatever her motivation, on some occasions, she could be too much to handle; and on this afternoon, she was just that.

Anna, thank God, was there to mediate her daughter's behavior. "Dearest, it's probably best not to work yourself up into a bother. Mary knew full well that smuggling letters out of her chambers would be a risk. Only she would be naïve enough to think those letters weren't being read."

"And you think that for *that*, she deserved to die? Many have done much more to Elizabeth and lived. She died for who she was, not for what she did." Her face shone with tears and her body shook as she spoke.

"How is the family going to react to her death?" Weary of Montpensier's theatrics, I asked Anna directly.

"There should be a memorial service, one fitting a Dowager Queen of France." From her purse, Montpensier pulled out a delicately embroidered handkerchief. Blowing her nose in the most ladylike manner possible, she remained silent for a moment.

Anna was also silent for a few moments. "We cannot make any public statement; only the king can speak about her death. We have the option of holding a quiet memorial service for Mary." Although she chose her words carefully, I knew that Anna felt relieved that her royal niece was finally no longer proving so troublesome on the international scene. The political future of France was precarious enough without being called on to help the Scots.

"My brothers will have to come to Paris for the service," Montpensier cut in. Neither Henri nor his younger brother, the Duc de Mayenne, had returned to Paris since my husband stormed out of our courtyard a year ago, taking the bulk of the French forces with him. His prolonged absence was disquieting for me; we had spent long periods apart since we married seventeen years earlier, but *this* absence had the ring of permanence.

"I must leave with the queen, she's planning a pilgrimage to the Abbey d'Ardenne, and she's ordered me to accompany her." At this, Montpensier's eyebrows lifted in surprise.

"Louise is going to Normandy? I can't believe the king would allow it."

"I'm to go as a hostage, guaranteeing her safe passage. If the League dares attack her, I'll be at risk."

Montpensier rolled her eyes and the handkerchief in her hands balled up into a wisp of material. Her knuckles went white, and I stared at her hand in fascination. "Now, the Guise are being used as human shields. Whatever will Henri Valois think of next, Mother?"

$\maltese$ 3 $\maltese$

The trip to Abbey d'Ardenne was a short one, lasting just over a week. Even with my presence as a hostage, the king seemed loath to risk Louise's life out in the Guise controlled northern reaches of his kingdom. By the twelfth, we were back in Paris, nearly dead with exhaustion. I trudged up to my chamber at the Hotel de Guise to find a message from Montpensier waiting for me. The family had arranged a public memorial and they would hold it the following morning. As the Duchess of Guise, it required my presence. I collapsed into bed and slept the sleep of the dead.

The memorial for Mary Stuart was nothing short of a canonization of a saint. They extolled the late queen's virtues, conveniently omitting any of her faults or propensity for scheming. No one, for example, bothered to mention that many people believed that she had been behind the murder of her second husband, Lord Darnley. Darnley had sired her son, who was now the very Catholic heir to the English throne. Priest after priest pointed out Mary's unswerving loyalty to the Catholic church and her determination to bring Scotland from heresy in following the scoundrel John Knox. Had Mary taken the English throne, they argued, England would have a faithful Catholic monarch and they would not threaten France with an invasion from the English.

As Mary's closest French relatives, Montpensier and her brother the Cardinal de Guise stood and accepted the condolences from the people who packed the church. When I first heard of the service, I assumed that it would be a private family affair. When I lifted my veil to see the assembled crowd, I noticed that many of them were strangers and that many of them were of the merchant and lower classes. This service was much more than a remembrance, it was a rally to the Catholic cause and a recruiting tool for the League. As I had suspected, neither my husband nor his brother, Mayenne, bothered to leave the field to come to Paris for the service. Montpensier used the opportunity to speak with every person she could, working the crowd like a master politician.

"I cannot believe neither Henri nor Mayenne are here," she hissed at me after the service once the crowds had thinned. In a corner, I saw two priests accepting coins from mourners. Not only was the service, raising support for the League, it was also raising money.

"They're busy commanding the army, Catherine. They can't take a day off to ride to Paris on a whim."

At my last word, she bristled. I immediately regretted saying it, since it would set her off. "My brothers are the leaders of the League in France, are they not? They lead the people since the king failed to do so."

"And if your brothers don't lead, who will take their place? You?" Had I expected her to demure and claim to be just a background actor, I was sadly mistaken. She instead straightened her spine and looked around us with pride. "Every son or daughter of Lorraine does their part in helping the family. Am I to do less because of my sex?" There was her naked ambition, on display for anyone to see. Henri's sister was becoming more dangerous and I would have to warn him he was in danger of a coup within his own house.

My husband must have sensed the coming schism within the Guise and Lorraine ranks because, in May, we were all called to Joinville for a family conference. These family conferences were a regular occurrence, happening frequently to ensure that the family acted with one voice. The family worked to ensure that each member, even the youngest daughter of the youngest son, felt as if they were as important to the family's success as the heir. The sense of camaraderie and appreciation made it easy to ensure loyalty generation after generation. Unlike most great families, who squabbled over scraps of inheritance, the Guise ensured that each member felt well taken care of. This ensured loyalty and had so far, kept the family from breaking apart.

After the death of the first Duchesse de Guise, my husband's grandmother and the woman who virtually raised me, that assurance of family loyalty was in danger of splintering. If the Guise were to challenge the king for failing to provide leadership for all of France, we could not afford to disintegrate into petty squabbling. Thus, I approached the opulent chateau of Joinville with trepidation on that warm May morning. Returning there was bittersweet for me because although I had been the Duchesse de Guise since my marriage in 1570, I was the mistress at Joinville in name only. Every man and woman in France knew that Antoinette of Bourbon ran the chateau and that fact was perfectly fine with me. I had no resentment for my formidable grandmother-in-law; she was virtually my grandmother. Along with a slew of young French noblewomen, I grew up under her care and I learned everything I knew about being a woman and wife at her knee. I was closer to Antoinette than my husband, who barely spent time at Joinville, or in his grandmother's presence.

In the long colonnade, I found my hawking husband slumped over the tall windows. "How did you arrive here before I did?"

He gave me a brilliant smile, "My horse was faster. Plus, I didn't have a retinue and furniture slowing me down." I had missed his gentle teasing. We had an unusual relationship, one that had allowed us to weather two decades of marriage. Neither of us came to our marriage bed an innocent, and neither begrudged the other for finding companions outside of that marriage bed. Unlike most wives, I did not trail after my husband in hysterics when I discovered him cheating. Nor did I follow the dictum I must act a prude and suffer in silence when news of my husband's infidelity reached my ears. I truly did not mind

Henri's affair with Charlotte de Sauve, but for the danger she posed in acting as a royal spy, she did not threaten me.

The danger that concerned me, however, was Montpensier's behavior the past few months. "I think you should do something about your sister."

He snorted, "Can you do something about your sister?" He had a point; my older sister Henriette and her husband Louis had refused public committing to the League for years. Henri had done all that he could to convince both of them, writing to Henriette several times to ask for her help. My sister feared if they declared for the League, it would spell the end of Louis' career as an advisor to the king. Given the fact that it composed the rest of the king's advisors of his toadying Mignons, Henriette might have a point. It was not in either of our natures to moderate, but perhaps, in the event of a disaster, we would need a moderate to plead before the king on our behalf. I hoped that we never came to that point.

"She's becoming more radical with each passing day. I think your mother has lost her ability to reign her in."

He turned towards me, his eyes betraying the weight of his responsibility of leading the Catholic League. "I need someone with her passion in the capital. Paris is the king's city, and she's much more effective than I am in subverting his policies." At my cocked head, he held up his hand, "As a woman, she can always plead she is of the weaker sex if the king comes after her. What kind of tyrant would he be if he threw a widow in the dungeon of Vincennes? The backlash would be more than the king could counter."

"She's whittling away your control of the League. She's too emotionally unstable to control its activities in Paris."

"And I cannot afford to be in Paris. If I leave the field, the king will immediately put Joyeuse or Épernon in charge of the army and I'll lose command forever. Besides, the king would not hesitate to throw me in prison. I don't have a woman's constitution to save me." At those words, his eyes raked over me. I had missed that part of our relationship, too. Taking a few steps, I laid my head on his shoulder. He encircled me with his arms and we made our way towards his chamber.

THE BALLROOM OF JOINVILLE BURST WITH LORRAINE AND GUISE cousins, with parents standing with their families. With so many of us crammed in there, the buzzing noise was deafening. "Aunt, my governess says it's time I retire." My younger sister, Marie's daughter and my namesake, Catherine, placed her hand softly on my forearm. I searched her face for any trace of her homely father, the Prince de Condé, but luckily, I only saw my late sister in her features.

"It's family only, I'm afraid. But next time you may be over there, seated behind the Duchesse de Lorraine." It was a tempting prospect, linking my niece in marriage to the heir of Lorraine. So far, we could not come to terms with Lorraine, but Catherine was only twelve. There was plenty of time to settle her future. Unlike me, I would not force her to marry as soon as she turned twelve, packed off to marry a complete stranger who followed a heretic faith.

I sighed at the thought. So far, she had shown no affinity towards the Calvinist teachings of her father. Marie grew up in a heretic household, under the care of our Aunt, Queen Jean of Navarre. Marie had escaped in time and converted to Catholicism and I would do all in my power to ensure that her daughter remained loyal to the church. There was no family in France more dedicated to the church of Rome and that was why the assembled Guise cousins were here for this most recent family meeting.

As I took my seat, I noticed a conspicuous absence in the room. "Where is Aumale?" The Duc of Aumale was one of my husband's many first cousins and one of his most trusted lieutenants in the League. In his youth, he served as the master of the king's Hunt and his tracking skills made him one of the most effective men in Henri's confidence.

"He's staying in Boulogne," the Duc d'Elbeuf cut in. He was yet another of my husband's first cousins and had I not grown up amongst the Guise, I would never have a chance of keeping them all straight.

"Why?"

"To win and hold it for the League. When the English try to invade France, we can defeat them at Boulogne." The port stood at the northern border of France, facing the English coast. If the English could capture the city, they could quickly make inroads towards the interior of France. Holding Boulogne meant stopping an English incursion before it started.

Even amongst family, Henri and his subordinates never spoke of a strategy so openly. They must be confident they can capture Boulogne and hold it. I glanced at Henri, who swept the room with a long glance before straightening the papers in his hand. "We have little time to tarry here in Joinville. I'm glad you could all take the time out to be here." A murmur of agreement rumbled across the room. None of the Guise were much for speeches and it did not surprise me that my husband immediately got to the point of the meeting.

"We need to hold every beachhead in Normandy. Phillip of Spain has done what Henri Valois will not do, avenge the death of our cousin, Mary." The entire room stopped to make the sign of the cross in unison. There was no more devoutly Catholic family in France than the Guise. "Phillip is building an armada to invade and conquer England. With Elizabeth as his prisoner, we will finally be able to stop the Protestant threat against France."

Behind me, I could hear astonished gasps for a few seconds. A thunderous applause quickly replaced those gasps. The Lorraine and Guise relations stood firmly behind the idea of justice for the Queen of Scots. Once the room had quieted down, Henri got to his next point.

"Aumale and I have promised Phillip that France will provide any safe harbor for beached Spanish galleons. While the king may balk at assuring Phillip of his support, the houses of Lorraine and Guise will stand with Catholic Spain."

"And does Phillip envision many ships running aground during this endeavor?" A deep male voice asked from the middle of the room.

"Nothing is certain, but in case of a shipboard accident, we and our allies are to give them succor. Be sure to tell all the men in your counties and duchies that. All the Guise will aid Spain in this holy mission."

"If Spanish troops run aground in France, there is no guarantee they will not loot and attack our lands," another male voice shouted from the back of the room. At this, Henri sighed.

"To make it to the Channel, they will have to sail around the

French coast. Spanish galleons are too well built to encounter much trouble. I doubt that we'll see much of the Spanish troops. This is simply to give Phillip a guarantee of our friendship."

"And what will Phillip give us for our 'friendship'?" Henri had not expected this many suspicious questions. His skin was getting mottled at the neck and around his ears. Two decades of marriage had taught me he was close to exploding from annoyance.

"Phillip will break the back of England and stop the Protestant troops that threaten to sail to France. The Swiss march from the east, which I need not remind you is close to here." He was right, Joinville was at the eastern edges of France and dangerously close to Switzerland. If Navarre and Condé wished, they could march into Champagne and threaten the city of Nancy. There were far too many Lorraine and Guise relations living in Champagne, and the thought of invading Protestant troops sent a shiver of terror through all of them.

"Then, who will protect us in the East? At least leave Mayenne here to guard his own family!" At that, panic swirled around the room and Henri put up his hands to stem it.

"Henri Valois will interpret any large force of troops in Champagne as a revolt against him. Since I have legitimate control over all French forces, I will station them in a manner as to protect all of France, not just us. Besides, once Aumale secures Boulogne for Spain, he will block a third of the troops threatening to land on French soil. With our forces strengthening Boulogne, the Spanish can afford to send troops in case Navarre or Condé attack. That is why we have to protect and hold Normandy: if we secure our shores, the Protestants cannot penetrate the heartland of France. That," he looked pointedly around the room, "is why we are all here. We have to display the unity that France itself has failed to show. We are the front line for our church and for our nation. The king and the Valois have betrayed their responsibility towards the nation. As Frenchmen and descendants of the Capets, it falls to us to defend France."

At that, the room fell silent. For the rest of the meeting, the Lorraine and Guise relations closed ranks and made plans to maintain their unified front against Protestants within the country and those threatening from without it. Before I left, I went to the wing of the chateau that had housed generations of noble girls across France. I had grown up there and now my goddaughter, Catherine occupied my old chamber. I found her sitting quietly, reading at her window.

"Isn't it still too cold to sit there?" The mid-March sun gave sufficient light, but not much warmth. She had placed a shawl that my sister Henriette sent from Paris around her shoulders.

"Probably." She gave me a smile and scooted over to allow me to sit next to her.

"I hear that my father is threatening to head towards Nancy, is that true?" Catherine rarely asked about her father. After Marie died, days after her birth, we could not bother Henry Bourbon with the newborn girl she left behind. She had never even seen her father and I wonder if he ever spared a thought for her. My husband had asked her to call him "Papa," which helped both of us recover from the loss of our daughter months before Catherine's birth. As a result, we thought of ourselves as Catherine's true parents.

I cleared my throat, stalling for time. Deciding that truth was the best policy, I turned to her. "We don't know where or when the Protestants will attack. Every report the Duc, your Papa, receives, tells him they plan to meet up with the troops coming from Switzerland. But don't worry," I placed my palm under her chin and realized that she was crying, "if that horrible man comes near you, your Papa will save you."

"I don't want to see that man," she shook her head and sobbed harder. I pulled her into a hug and held her, while she continued to cry. "No matter what they say, I don't support him. I don't want him to win. I'm a good Catholic, just like you and Papa taught me. I'm not a spy."

She dissolved into heaving sobs and my blood ran cold. Suddenly, I remembered myself at her age, married to a rabid Protestant. My first husband had tried to make me promise that I would never marry Guise. I refused to make that promise. Still, months after my marriage, there were Guise relations who looked down at me with suspicion. Someone accused me of being a spy for the followers of Calvin. I took years to win their trust and my heart ached at my niece facing the same torment.

"Are there people here who are questioning your faith or your loyalty?" She was silent and her refusal to answer me told me all that I needed to know. Fury ran through me. I held her for a quarter of an hour, refusing to leave her until I felt satisfied that she was better. Closing the door to her chamber softly, I padded down the hall to the chamber occupied by the governess, Madame Longrais.

❧

I FOUND HER SITTING AT A TABLE, PLAYING CARDS WITH ONE OF THE upstairs maids. When they saw me, they both leaped to their feet. "Madame, I will speak with you. You," I gave the maid a withering look before she could scurry away, "will report to the Chamberlain." After she made her retreat, I whirled on Madame Longrais. "How long have you served at this house, Madame?"

She swallowed, "For ten years, My Lady."

"And how would you rate your term here as a governess?" She trembled before me. I may have a quick temper, but I am not fond of playing with another woman as a cat plays with a mouse. Still, the knowledge that the other girls had been tormenting my niece under her own nose enraged me.

"I would think you and the Duc feel pleased with how I have been managing the girls since the death of Duchesse Antoinette." She fell silent.

I would get right to the point, "My niece tells me that the other girls accuse her of being a heretic and a spy for the Prince de Condé. Are you aware of this?"

"No, Madame," she shook her head violently, her voice barely above a whisper.

"Yet, it is your duty to supervise the girls, is it not?"

"My Lady, I cannot watch the girls every minute of the day or night. It's possible they are harassing your niece at night after Vespers. You and I both know how sneaky young girls can be."

I knew all too well. Charlotte de Sauve skulked around France, winding her white limbs around my husband's body every chance she could get. I had no evidence that the woman was purposefully shirking her duties. The girls at the dormitory of Joinville were more covert than I had imagined. They could have picked Catherine out as a weak girl and saved their torture for when there were no adults around.

"I will ask for you to send reports of my niece's progress every month. I expect to hear of no more incidents of teasing and name-calling. Any girl caught doing so will be sent home. I don't care how valuable a client she is to the Guise family, there is no room for an ill-mannered girl in my home." I made a note to have Catherine send me regular reports and through a system that Madame Longrais would have no access to. I would not give her the opportunity to dictate what Catherine said in her private correspondence.

❧ 4 ❧

Before Summer ended, I saw Montpensier's point of view. While most of my previous dealings with the movement of the Protestant forces had been theoretical and far removed, as fall came, their presence became all too real. I felt the panic and terror of their presence the other Catholics had felt for months. In the sultry heat of July, the king and my husband met at Meaux, in the middle of France, to discuss the advance of troops across France. Many of the generals thought the Protestants would attack in any corner of the country, putting every Frenchman at risk. Others, including the king believed the Protestants were hellbent on marching towards Lorraine to strike at the heart of Guise holdings.

I was only four months into my latest pregnancy. This would be the twelfth time I would carry Henri of Guise's child within my body. While I was far from a fragile woman, the constant strain on my body was getting to me. I was almost thirty and had spent far too much of my life with child. This child would likely be my last pregnancy. I had five living children, more than enough to carry the Guise line forward for many generations. If I had thought I could sit quietly while my child grew inside me, I was very much mistaken.

On the afternoon of September 2nd, I sat beside the king and

Queen Louise, while they listened to a lecture about philosophy from an Italian orator. The irony of the king sitting and listening to a lecture about something so frivolous while he ignored counsel about the state of his nation, infuriated me, but years at court meant that I could hide my anger behind a mask of tranquility. Half an hour into the lecture, one of the king's Swiss Guards crept in and whispered in his royal ear. The king rose and left the room abruptly. As the orator looked helplessly towards Queen Louise to see if he should continue, she indicated that we were to take a break. Thankful for the respite, I excused myself to attend to my toilet.

As I walked back along the corridors of the Louvre, I saw Charlotte de Sauve coming in my direction. I tried to alter my course to avoid her, but she appeared to be seeking me out.

"The king is on his way to arrest Montpensier's creatures I hear," The words sounded casual, but I could tell she was baiting me.

"Creatures? Whatever are you talking about Madame de Sauvé?"

"It's Madame de Noirmoutier. Perhaps you haven't heard of my recent marriage." She had married the Marquis de Noirmoutier, elevating her status at court and making her a richer woman than ever before, yet she still saw fit to pursue my husband.

"Ah, yes—I think I heard something about you buying a new husband. Perhaps this one won't steal from you." I hoped that this little dig would cause her to leave in disgust, but I was not so lucky.

"Aren't you afraid that I'll implicate you in Montpensier's schemes?" Charlotte batted her long eyelashes at me. Unlike most of us, she was a natural blonde. She never had to dye her hair to achieve the delicate coloring that men at court found irresistible. Feeling bloated at my pregnancy, I felt ungainly beside her, flaring my anger even further.

"Madame, you never have bothered to tell me what your personal politics are. Do you support the church that nurtured you since birth, or do you continue to consort with Heretics?"

"Me?" her voice dripped venom. "I have always remained loyal to the same faith, unlike you, who changes religions like you change husbands." The old taunts from childhood came back the lifelong Catholics insinuating that I was a traitor to both sides. Common sense told me to hurry back to the queen's side and away from a further confrontation with the tart standing in front of me. Unfortunately, I used none of my common sense.

"Ah, loyalty. I suppose that you remain a Valois spy. Tell me, who do you work for? The Queen Mother? The king? When you're rolling around in someone else's sheets, who pays your bills?"

She opened her mouth to respond, but a matron told us that the queen required our presence. She denied me the chance to learn who was pulling Charlotte de Sauve's purse strings.

✦

DAYS LATER, I RECEIVED A LETTER FROM MY HUSBAND. THE KING had ordered him to move all French troops to Gien, a village within my sister's Duchy of Nevers. "The king believes the Protestants march straight for Joinville," he wrote in a hastily scrawled note. "You will be safe as far away from Champagne as you can get, either at Eu or with your sister at Nevers." His letter gave me two options: return to my chateau in Normandy or visit my sister at our ancestral home in Nevers. Since Henriette had resigned from Queen Louise's service eight years ago, we rarely had time to spend with one another. I was still in the early days of my pregnancy before the added weight made me unwieldy. I decided that it was the perfect time to make a sisterly visit.

After a long, bumpy ride over muddy roads, I finally pulled into the courtyard of the Ducal Palace of Nevers as Jeanne buzzed excitedly beside me. Renee had outgrown the nursery, and I had sent her to Joinville. The last time I was at the Palace, I was about to marry Antoine de Croy, the Prince de Porcien. Barely out of childhood, all I could think of was the brilliant life I was about to partake upon. On that warm afternoon, however, I had returned there for protection.

Henriette met me at the top of the steps and embraced me. "Guise was smart to send you away from Joinville. From what I've heard, the king expects there to be a major engagement outside of Joinville. There are German and Swiss mercenaries camped outside of the village. He's hoping that Guise will fall during the battle and all of his worries will be over."

I snorted, "He really thinks if my husband dies, all of his worries will be over? What a naïve man! If Henri falls, there are plenty of League members ready to avenge him. Phillip will still plan to invade France, but he will solicit a less reasonable man to aid him. At least my husband knows how to keep Spain at bay. A traitor may take a small Spanish payment and sell us all out."

We came to a small boy, one who looked as if he could be my son, Charles. The thought brought a pang of longing to see my firstborn who waited out the Protestant threat behind the safety of abbey walls. Henri and I had moved him to an abbey deep within Lorraine, where his uncle, the Cardinal de Guise, could keep a watchful eye on him. This Charles was Henriette's son and heir, who was all of eight years old.

"Charles, would you like to play with your cousin, Jeanne?" Henriette's voice showed that she expected him to say a quick yes and leave the two of us to speak in private. Charles foiled her plans, however, by vehemently shaking his head.

"She's too small." He curled his upper lip in disgust at the task asked of him. Henriette rolled her eyes in response.

"Show her the staircase, please. It is the birthright of every Cleves child to run up and down the staircase until exhaustion sets in. You would not deny your young cousin the pleasure of doing so, would you? What kind of gentleman would you be?"

The maternal guilt worked its way on Charles and chastened, he nodded. "Okay, Mama. Here," he held out his hand to Jeanne, who looked at me in confusion. "Go ahead, you'll love it." She slowly let go of my skirts and walked towards her cousin. With our children gone, we sat in the palace's solarium to speak in private.

"Louis tells me that the king thinks all the Protestant incursions are attacks against the League, not him."

"Does he think he has no enemies then? That this is just another battle between warring faiths? This is not another St. Bartholomew's Day. The same people who would not think of betraying King Charles have no problem with rebelling against the current king."

"The king sees himself as the embodiment of Catholicism in France. You know how publicly he wears his faith, self-flagellating and going on as many pilgrimages as possible."

"Spectacles are hardly a way to prove that he is a loyal Catholic," I rolled my eyes at the thought of the king working so hard to convince his Catholic subjects he had the situation well in hand. Everyone knew that there was a schism between the throne and the rest of the Holy Church. He was fooling no one.

"He'll ignore his Catholic critics and when it comes time to place the blame, he'll claim that they're Protestants determined to undermine his reign." She stopped and looked at me, "As far as Louis and I are concerned, the only rebellion against the king is foreign and Protestant."

☙❧

I settled into my ancestral home in Nevers, determined to make as little trouble for my sister as possible. Hoping to call little attention to myself, I had only taken Jeanne and two of my maids on my trip from Paris. If Henriette saw I was not there to stir up dissension, then there would be little about my visit to object to. Her household was a small one, a holdover from the time she left court service. I envied her simplicity; our household comprised refugees, dissidents, soldiers, and radicals who flocked to the Guise banner. Those hangers-on meant extra expenditures, straining the paltry pension we received from Phillip of Spain.

While I worked to avoid Henriette's bad temper, others did not. The city of Nevers was much more compact than sprawling Paris and the cathedral was directly behind the Ducal Palace, allowing Jeanne and I to attend Mass daily. As we exited the cathedral, a young man dressed in the simple garb of a Jesuit stopped to speak with us. "Madame de Guise, I heard that you were here in Nevers and I wanted to thank you personally for your patronage of our order in Normandy."

Henri's Jesuit mission in Eu was his idea and one I strongly disagreed with, but the fresh-faced boy standing in front of me need not know that. "We see it as our duty to help those who are fighting to preserve the sanctity of our church." I turned to walk past him, but he stopped me.

"Would it be too much to impose upon you to visit at the palace tomorrow? There is something I need to speak to you about." The request seemed innocent enough, so I gave him an indulgent shrug. "Meet me tomorrow afternoon."

The young priest was punctual, appearing at the palace gates well before our appointment. Interpreting his punctuality as a sign of respect, I welcomed him into Henriette's salon and we settled into small talk. Father Jean began his career in the church in a small village in Normandy, hoping to improve his family's fortunes by joining the Jesuit order. A quarter of an hour into our interview, he came to the point of his visit.

"My Lady, I realize I have no right to take advantage of your charity, but I am desperate. I need your help."

Lured into a sense of ease, I lifted my eyebrows and urged him to continue. "I have two younger sisters remain trapped in England. My parents sent them abroad with me when I went to England to minister to the Catholics there. We were lured in by Elizabeth Tudor's promises of toleration of Catholics, but now–"

I held up my hand, horrified at the thought of two vulnerable children at the mercy of the English Protestants. "Are you not able to send for them?"

He shook his head vehemently. "No, with the Spanish threatening to attack the English coast at any moment, the sea captains are charging ten times what it usually costs for a voyage across the Channel. Once I have them safely in France, I can relax, but I can spirit them out of England."

"And you would like me to give you the money for their passage?" The after effects of Mass made me more charitable than good sense would have allotted, but I felt moved to pity for his plight.

"No, my Lady—I would only ask to *borrow* the money. I will pay you back in full." He looked so earnest and so naively hopeful for his family I could not say no to him.

"Very well—I will advance the money to you. Repay me when you can."

He stood and took my hand. Kissing it, he bowed his head to my hand. My pride was stroked at his reverence. By the end of the week, I had sent the money to the young priest, and he was back on his way from his order to Normandy.

Flushed with the elation of having done a small part to help the English Catholic refugees, I found it easy to sit with my sister. Freed from the endless demand of court duties, we could sit and talk as long as either of us wished. As Jeanne and her cousin Charles played in the palace's foyer, Henriette and I read over our niece, Marie's letters from Joinville.

"You're certain she's safe?" Although the Dowager Duchesse had supervised Marie's upbringing, each of us took our duties as surrogate mothers to our niece seriously since her birth. Nothing changed that fact.

I nodded, "Joinville is well-protected, it's just the road is at risk. Henri would not hear of my traveling along it from Paris. That man and his troops camp just outside of one of Lorraine's isolated abbeys." At the mention of "That Man," we both rolled our eyes in disgust. Time had done nothing to lessen our shared hatred of our former brother-in-law and cousin, Henry, Prince of Condé "He has another daughter now and I'm sure she'll be raised as a proper Protestant. Even if he did remember Marie, he's long since replaced her in his heart."

"He has a submissive wife now to do his bidding. He sequesters her in his chateau and refuses to allow her to court."

I shrugged, "She's really not missing anything by not attending court. It's dull without you." At that, Henriette gave me a small smile. When Henri Valois took the throne thirteen years earlier, it was a foregone conclusion that our youngest sister, Marie would sit beside him as his queen. He was a man in love, a king who would have made a strong ally. Today, we could only sit and remember the sister who left us thirteen years ago. "I sent Marie some silks for her birthday. She's a teenager this year, which means she's ready to be betrothed."

"Who does Guise want for her husband?" If Marie's mother was alive, she would lead this conversation. If her father had any honor or sense of decency, he would have already planned an advantageous marriage for his firstborn child.

"He still wants to marry her to one of Lorraine's sons. I support the match and if she's at Nancy, she won't be too far from us."

"Louis and I are thinking about one of Lorraine's daughters for Charles." I glanced at my nephew, who had taken to his duty to watch his younger cousin with a seriousness that was touching. A husband with such a protective nature was a find. There was a seriousness about the boy that seemed well beyond his years.

"I'll have Henri speak to Lorraine for you."

◈

ON SEPTEMBER 11TH, BEROU, THE CHAMBERLAIN WHO HAD SERVED the Ducal Palace of Nevers for longer than I could remember, came into the garden, holding a scrap of paper. Henriette and I were watching our children play and enjoying the cooler weather of early Fall. "Madame, I've bad news I'm afraid." He handed the message to Henriette, who let out a groan of frustration.

"What?" I turned from Jeanne, who struggled to use her dress as an apron for transporting pebbles.

"There's been a battle." At that, my blood ran cold. The Protestants had attacked Lorraine and could then turn directly towards Joinville. This would be a disaster for our family and the many retainers who sent their noble daughters for education at the chateau.

"It was at Coutras," Henriette clarified. I frowned; the name meant nothing. There was no place in the entire Champagne region named Coutras.

"It's in Burgundy, southeast of La Rochelle. Condé double-backed with most of his troops and headed towards the coast. They engaged royal troops under Joyeuse's command." I sent a quick word of thanks up to Heaven that my husband and his troops were safe.

"Well, that's good, isn't it? One of the king's favorites is dead. The bulk of the army is safely in Lorraine. How is that bad?"

Berou cut in, "My Lady, I'm sorry to say the Protestants had a rousing victory. They cut down Joyeuse's troops. And the army has not been in Lorraine for over a week. The king ordered them to march to Gien."

It dumbfounded me. "Why are they in Gien? That makes little sense." I searched Berou and Henriette's faces and he tried to explain the ramifications of the battle. "The king wanted to hold the Loire, so he chose Gien as the staging ground for the rest of the army a few days ago. Joyeuse's troops were a small portion of the army and most of them were young, untrained troops. Condé's men were too experienced for them. Someone injured Joyeuse so badly that no one expects him to live."

"And what of Lorraine? Is it safe?"

"The king purposefully left Lorraine exposed to Swiss and German troops. He would sacrifice Lorraine to the Protestants. It's likely that he hoped someone would kill Guise in the effort." The extent of the king's betrayal hit me, stoking my ire. He had purposefully tried to expose my husband to danger and deprive him of his own troops. I had not heard from Henri for days and suddenly I knew why.

"That's not all, I'm afraid." I looked at Henriette, who looked as if she could hear no more bad news, either, but she nodded, urging him on. "The Prince de Condé was injured and taken from the battlefield. Someone shot him off his horse, but the Protestants took him to his Chateau at St. Angely."

If I were a better Christian, I might offer thanks that my former brother-in-law was safe. Instead, I felt annoyed that this longstanding thorn in our side was still alive and capable of doing more harm to us.

"Well, at least Joyeuse is gone. That's one of the Mignons out of the government." Joyeuse was governor of Normandy, an honor usually given to princes of the blood, men far above his station. Men like my husband, who would have been a much more effective administrator of northern France. With Joyeuse dead, now perhaps the king would see reason and appoint Henri to the post. If the king would do so, I would feel safe in returning to my chateau in Eu without the threat of molestation from the king.

As soon as possible, I scribbled a letter to my husband in Lorraine, thinking he was deep in the western reaches of France. It was weeks before he replied, and I soon learned why. After learning of the debacle in Coutras and the king's betrayal, Henri had doubled-back towards Paris to rejoin the bulk of the army before the Protestants could destroy all French forces. Navarre, even without Condé at his side, was only days away from joining German reinforcements and creating a Protestant force so great that no royal troops could match it. Before Coutras, Henri could only shadow the Protestants near him in Lorraine and watch their movements. When the king took the bulk of his troops off to Gien, my husband was even more shorthanded than ever.

The advantage of having such a small force, however, was a greater mobility and Henri could outpace the Protestants until he could find a place to cleave their forces in two. He found that place halfway between Paris and the sacred city of Chartres just before November turned into December. Besides cutting down two-thousand Swiss mercenaries, he successfully plundered their supply train, one that destined for Navarre's troops. Holding the Swiss troops captive, my husband lay in wait for Navarre to reinforce the Swiss, but no help came for the invaders. As was typical of my cousin, Navarre, something much more appetizing than a victory distracted him; his newest mistress. For weeks, he delayed in his paramour's arms while waiting for Condé to recover. Navarre's dalliance gave my husband more than enough time to provision his troops and provide payment for them.

The bulk of the spoils in the Protestant camps came from the French countryside, mostly Guise and Lorraine lands. With his victory near Chartres, Henri could return many of the items plundered from his retainers, increasing the debt owed to him by the people of Lorraine.

As I read his letter, I beamed with pride. My husband had cut the main source of heretic troops from the West and they would be on their way back to Switzerland with nothing more than the clothes on their back. During their long march back, they would have to face the wrath of the common folk they had stolen from. He cut Navarre off, and the people turned against the Protestant marauders. This victory was enough to prove to the king that this use of German troops was ruinous to France. Doing so had turned the common people against him.

I had two short days to savor my husband's victory in central France, during which, the baby inside me became increasingly active. This latest child was due in the New Year, likely before the end of February. Many women hated to give birth in the coldest months of the year because the ice and snow made travel hazardous. With twelve births already behind me, I much preferred to go to my childbed during the winter. The swelling of my limbs and the stress on my body were too much to bear during the heat of the Summer. Unlike many women, I considered Winter to be the most fortuitous time of the year to bring a child into the world.

I still had a third of my pregnancy to endure and I was already waddling everywhere I went and the slightest exertion tired me. I likewise waddled into the dining room of the palace at the end of November to sup with my sister. My sister seemed distracted, but given her propensity to lose herself in her thoughts, I paid little mind to her odd behavior. After the servants cleared the dishes, she rose to her feet and strolled towards me, clutching a piece of paper.

"What is this?" She laid it beside me and I could only stare at it in confusion.

"I do not understand."

"You're right, you probably wouldn't know, so I'll tell you. It's a note from the forces stationed at Gien saying they've captured the spy you sent to Eu."

I could only stare at her, my mouth agape. "Spy? Have you lost control of your senses? I sent no spy to Eu. I sent no one, even a servant to collect rent." Knowing how greedy Joyeuse had been during his lifetime, I assumed that any of the money sent on the road from Eu his troops would raid to Nevers and immediately placed into his own pocket. The odious man knew nothing other than greed. Delaying my payment of the rents turned out to be a costly decision since my income had dwindled since he became governor of Normandy.

"Really, Catherine? You deny that you've been carrying out a rebellion against the king right under my nose the entire time?" Her face became darker and flushed with red as she spoke. Neither of us was blessed with olive complexions and the slightest amount of anger showed immediately on our skin. It terrified most people of the court when my sister became enraged, but most people were not her younger sister. I could easily hold my own in an argument with her. This time, however, I knew that I was innocent of whatever scheme she accused me of.

"Do you have any proof of any rebellion I've been carrying on? The only people I've seen since I got here are you and Charles. I suppose your eight-year-old son is my co-conspirator?" At the mention of Charles, she flew into a rage. I had gone too far, but it was too late to take back what I said.

"Proof?" she all but screamed the word at me, multiplying her anger. "Follow me and I will show you proof." She stormed out of the dining room and towards the study. I struggled to keep pace with her. In my state, walking was becoming difficult, and I had to stop frequently to catch my breath. Without a child in her belly, Henriette easily strode into the room before I could follow her. Once in the study, I took a seat to calm myself. While I did so, she rifled through a drawer until she found a stack of papers. "Here," she tossed them at me.

I scanned the papers, unwilling to believe what I was reading. Amongst my letters to the Father Jean, who had begged me for money to help spirit his young sisters from England to France were detailed reports between the Jesuits of Gien and Eu, exposing how the money was being funneled to pay for the League's defiance of the king. I had seen none of these letters, but as I read them, I realized that not a single sou of what I had sent would help innocent girls escape religious prosecution; it would instead pay for ammunition and supplies. My signature sat prominently at the bottom of every letter I sent to the young man.

"I am sorry, Henriette. He has exploited my charity. I did not understand what he was really doing with the money I gave him."

"You never asked for an accounting of the money? You're usually more careful than that. What has this League done to you?"

Likely, the League had made me as reckless as Montpensier. Yet, unlike her, I had the stresses of pregnancy to influence my bad decisions. The young man had preyed on my emotions when he spun a yarn of helpless girls looking for a savior. A pregnant woman was entirely too easy to exploit, and I had fallen for his scheme. He had successfully played me for a sentimental fool. I was ashamed at how gullible I had been.

In his letters, he expounded me as his patron and begged for more contributions in my name to add to what I had unwittingly donated to the cause. What I had contributed to the cause was a sizable sum, but according to these documents, the Jesuits had raised a considerable sum to finance their activities from Nevers to Normandy.

She sat beside me an exhaled a long sigh. "If it's any consolation, I believe you."

I nodded, unable to speak for a few moments. We sat in silence, neither of us able to break the awkwardness between us. After several moments, she spoke.

"I've spoken to Louis about this. Since it involves the king's troops in this, we really have no choice. I have to banish you from Nevers, or the king will see the two of us as being complicit in this scheme."

It horrified me at how easily she and Louis would throw me to the wolves. I was her only surviving sibling. "Banish! You must be joking with me. Where could I go? The Swiss troops have laid Lorraine to waste while Normandy is still rife with men loyal to Joyeuse."

"You should go to Paris. There is no threat of invasion there. The king is planning on returning to the Louvre within the week. You can go to plead your case to him in person. Louise will probably do all that she can to help you." She shrugged, "Well, all that Louise can do, anyway."

Return to Paris in disgrace, accused of conspiring against the king? And with no one to plead my case? I shook my head, "No, you're asking too much of me."

"Catherine, this is the second Jesuit conspiracy that has occurred under my roof. Neither Louis nor I can afford to anger the king before he suspects us. I have my son to protect. I cannot protect you too this time."

My sister was right; I had placed them all in danger with my naivety. The honorable thing would be to leave Nevers as soon as possible for Paris. Spite caused me to rebel against her, however. "Are you two still going to continue to play both sides? How much will that cost you in the long run?"

She whirled upon me. "You and Guise have already taken the part of radicals. What other parts are left to the rest of us? While you quarrel openly with the crown, the rest of France has to take sides and hope we make the right one. Do you really think if you were in our position, you would not try to travel a middle road?"

"No choice *is* a choice, Henriette! When are you and Louis going to realize that?"

"Catherine, Louis and I have made our decision. Nevers is our duchy, and this is our home. I expect you to honor our decision."

The next morning, with Jeanne beside me, I began the long journey towards Paris. Within the silent carriage, I had plenty of time to ponder my situation. In the past, I had watched as Montpensier stroked the fire of rebellion, all the while thinking of her as little more than a radical. Now events outside of my control branded as another radical, although I was innocent. They would know me for being a radical and a rebel, even while I had tried to tread my version of a middle way for myself. In a way, I had followed the same philosophy that Louis and Henriette had espoused for years. I had warned Henriette that no choice was a choice and my words were coming back to haunt me.

It was time for me to take a more active role in promoting the League. It was too late to turn back. Henriette showed me I had no other option. It was time to enjoy the perks of being a radical leader. At those thoughts, the child within me stirred, and I felt a mother's guilt wash over me. With one daughter not yet out of the nursery and a child coming in a few months, I had no business contemplating an active rebellion against the king. As a childless widow, Montpensier had that luxury. I had children to protect and their future to safeguard, just as Henriette had banished me to safeguard her son's future. Sighing, I laid my head back on the upholstered bench and tried to lure myself to sleep. I would have trouble enough once I reached Paris.

Ispent several days nursing my wounded pride before I ventured to leave my chambers at the Hotel de Guise. Henriette might well have a point I would have to grovel before the king eventually, but I had no desire to head to the Louvre to see if the king had heard of my supposed seditious activity. Still, with the Advent season, my presence at court was a requirement. The more Guise women were absent, the more the king would think a conspiracy surrounded him.

I found Queen Louise in her privy chamber, as serene as usual. She had none of the excitable fervor of most of the Lorraine dynasty and this was one occasion that I was glad for that fact. "My Madame de Guise—how was your trip to Nevers?"

Before I could stop myself, I blurted out, "Someone framed me for committing a conspiracy. My sister banished me from her home." I don't know why I said such a thing to her, I can only think it was because of pregnancy moods. I shamed myself immediately afterward by breaking down and crying like a fishwife. The matrons in the room rose to cluck over me and Louise took my hand. "Catherine, if someone falsely accused you, that is terrible. Tell me what happened; maybe, I can speak to the king for you."

I told her the truth of the young priest who preyed upon my

sympathy and the discovery of his notes. She nodded and rubbed my forearm as I blubbered on. The more of the tale I told, the more emotional I became. I hope to God that this was only because of my pregnancy. "I'll talk to the king at supper. Don't worry about this and don't let it spoil the miracle of your coming child."

I could only bite my lip as I tried to compose myself. Louise pressed further, "If it would make you feel better, it would honor me if you would name me as the child's godmother."

Her offer was touching, but Henri and I had already talked about the naming of a godmother of our next son or daughter. "Queen Margot has already agreed to serve as godmother. Please don't think I am in such severe straits."

She smiled, "Then, this little one will have two queens for godmothers. He or she will be twice blessed." I could not refuse her offer to be an additional godmother for my child and as godmother, she would have a greater stake in intervening with the king for me. I nodded and thanked her for her generosity.

Louise was true to her word, going against her usual reticence to convince the king that someone had framed me in the payments for the English emigres. The king, usually an aloof man, even took the time to be solicitous throughout the Advent celebrations. Perhaps, it was the celebration of the birth of our Lord that put him in such a charitable mood. Whatever his reasons, I was thankful for it.

DECEMBER WAS NOT PEACEFUL FOR EVERY MEMBER OF MY FAMILY, however. Henri remained in the field, trying his best to stem his frustration with the king's behavior. Behind my husband's back, the king gave the Swiss mercenaries extra money to slink back to Switzerland unmolested by Guise troops. Money that should have gone to provisioning Henri's army, went instead to paying off foreign heretics. My husband's fury was so great I was thankful I was not there in person to see it. He wrote long letters raging over the king's betrayal. In a little of bittersweet revenge, Henri took the Duke of Lorraine's son with him across the Swiss border where the two set fire to as many Protestant villages as possible before returning to the safety of a devastated Lorraine.

My belly continued to expand and other than light duties for the queen, there was little I could do, whether purposefully aiding the League's activities. Montpensier more than made up for me in vexing the king. She had been living on borrowed time since the previous June when she and her coconspirators put up the mural damming Elizabeth Tudor. I suppose the king ran out of Christian charity after forgiving me because he chose December 1587 to bring finally Montpensier to heel. When I was on my journey back from Nevers, the king attempted to rout all the men on her payroll, raiding houses of Leaguers across Paris. The raid was a complete failure and the people of Paris flocked to the bridge over the Seine connecting the Sorbonne to the Ile de Cite. If Épernon had his way, they would fill the scaffolds with the hanging bodies of conspirators, but the king instead, banished most of the priests and men who had been acting in Montpensier's name. She found herself with few people surrounding her, but the population continued to be restless. In December, the rector of the Sorbonne declared that it was within church law to depose such princes who acted in a way that endangered the church.

This was pushing the king too far. On December 16th, as we were about to sit to listen to a Christmas concert, the king strode into the room, his face as heated as Henriette's had been when throwing me out of her home in Nevers. Before taking his seat beside Queen Louise, he fixed a cruel stare directly at me. "Madame de Guise, I assume you have heard of the scheming going on here in Paris. My beloved wife," he nodded to Louise, who blushed in return, "tells me you are innocent of these rebellions, but I cannot say the same for other members of the House of Lorraine."

Dear God, please let this have nothing to do with Montpensier, I prayed. I hadn't spoken or written to her in weeks. This time, not only was I innocent, there was no written proof in my hand to damn me. If someone implicated me in Montpensier's latest activities, the worst that could happen would be to place me in the dungeons of Vincennes. Even if the king was guilty of the abominations, the most radical League members accused him of, he would never stoop so low as to harm a pregnant woman. If there were any who were undecided about their loyalty to the king, such a heinous act would make their decision for them. He and I knew that.

"I am told that Montpensier pays the curates of Paris to speak against me during their homilies. They say I was so jealous of your husband's victories I agreed with the Heretics who invaded our nation. Do you believe what they are saying, Madame?"

I folded my hands in my lap. Or at least, where my lap used to be, and tried to adopt the pose of a serene Madonna. "Sire, it is probably best to remember that Montpensier has none of the comforts of marriage you and I enjoy. She lost her husband, and you cannot imagine the sorrow of losing a spouse." I glanced at Queen Louise, my voice heavy with innuendo. "Even worse, she has no children of her own. There is no one in her vast home to provide her with comfort or companionship. I assume she does what she does because she wants to put her passions into something. She is misguided, but then, as a woman, I know how difficult it is to resist the being swayed by emotions." I lifted my hands and shrugged, hoping that the king would see her as a harmless woman shouting from her salon. It was a long shot, but I felt determined to do anything.

"There is also talk of your husband taking a trip to Rome. Has he spoken to you of such a thing?" His words shocked me, I had heard nothing of Henri leaving France. As commander of French forces, it would be career suicide to leave the troops for someone else to assume command.

"Rome? No. Our child is due in two months. Henri wouldn't dare leave me for such a long journey with another child on the way." It was a weak excuse; the king was afraid that Henri would go to Rome to beg to have him deposed just as the rector from the Sorbonne was preaching to the crowds. I had to convince him that the rumor was nothing more than poisonous gossip.

"At any rate, I plan to go to Normandy once the child is born. I would like to show him or her my chateau at Eu."

"I hear it is a lovely structure you are building. I shall advise The Duc d'Épernon he should visit once he settles in as governor of Normandy." I inwardly groaned; we had just gotten rid of Joyeuse and now the king was installing his remaining favorite in his place? No sooner than Joyeuse's body was cold, the king had named him the Governor of Normandy. Would the king never learn that his actions had no consent from the people he governed? My husband deserved the governorship of Normandy. No one in France was better qualified to rule the north. This was a punishment for the Guise dominance in the North. The king was determined to break our backs.

۞

Christmas and the New Year continued without more discord between the king and the Leaguers. I assumed that the king had forgotten Montpensier and her agents until I heard rumors they were comparing the king to Edward II of England and his lover Piers Gaveston. An accusation of sodomy was going entirely too far and the first week of January 1588, the king once again called Montpensier to his presence at the Louvre. Anna offered to accompany her daughter, hoping that her presence there would soften the king's wrath, but Montpensier refused to take her with her into her private audience. Anna and I walked with her as far as the great doors to the king's audience chamber. "Ah, the Queen of Paris is here," the king's chamberlain snorted at her with derision. Not a woman to fall prey to be intimidation Montpensier looked at him without saying a word.

"I believe we need to get some fresh air," Anna declared loudly, as the heavy door closed in front of us. She gently tugged me beside her, doing her best to support my swollen body as we walked towards an alcove.

"I've done all that I can do to beg the king's mercy; I'm out of options at this point," her voice edged with anger, as she whispered in my ear while we walked past curious courtiers.

"Has the Queen Mother been able to make any headway with the king?" Anna and Catherine de Medici were friends from their earliest days in France. Despite both having noble French heritage, the French nobles saw them both as Italian interlopers after decades at court. Their shared battles for legitimacy at court made them lifelong allies.

It was this friendship that kept the Guise and Valois from tearing each other apart for years.

She shook her head, the strain of dealing with her only daughter written on her face. "Even they are more estranged than ever. The king refuses to listen to her counsel, and he disregards her experience. He'd rather listen to those hayseeds from the wilds of the provinces. Country folk are so adept at handling statecraft." She rolled her eyes in disgust and was silent for a few moments. Desperate to break the silence, I turned to her.

"I think your daughter is the most extreme example of how weary we all are of the king's favoritism towards these nobodies. We are all suffering while the country is being run by inept governors. Meanwhile, we're dealing with enough droughts and crops to ruin us. I can't blame her for her frustration."

She arched an eyebrow, "You sound like you agree with her methods."

"Not so much her methods as her sentiments." I let out a long sigh. "I do, however, agree with her frustration. Paris has been boiling for months." A guard walked by and I lowered my voice so only Anna could hear me. "When the city goes into open revolt, we have to have a family capable of ruling and directing the people so that the country won't fall into chaos. The moment France falls into chaos, we're easy pickings for Spanish or English invasion."

"Take care how you say things like that. You sound like you're advocating a Guise-led rebellion against the throne."

"Me?" I turned to her in shock, "I'm the size of my house and I can barely move around. What can I do in this condition? Have you ever heard of a revolution being led by a heavily pregnant woman?" I rubbed my aching back, which refused to let up and give me some relief.

"At the moment, I'm worried about my daughter attempting to lead a revolution. If the king--" she stopped as the doors to the Presence Chamber swung open and Catherine of Lorraine, Duchesse de Montpensier strode out, barely concealing a smug smile. "Mother, Sister." She greeted us as if we were simply standing idly by at a ball.

"So?" Anna hissed in her ear and strode behind her, trying to match her pace. Catherine gave a delicate shrug in reply. Left to myself, I waddled behind them as quickly as I could manage in my state.

I finally caught up with mother and daughter in Anna's chambers, where they were deep in an argument. "You assume too much weakness on the king's part. It doesn't matter how weak he is he can have your head removed from your body with just a flick of his hand." Anna paced as she lectured her daughter, who looked unmoved by her mother's words of warning.

"That's just what you don't understand, Henri Valois knows that if he were to put a Guise in prison, the revolt he fears will begin immediately. He can't afford to do anything. That is how weak he has become. With every noble in France alienated from him and the populace convinced he is consorting with the Antichrist, he has no one to come to his defense."

I took a seat, determined not to receive any of the anger that existed between the two women. As I sat, the weariness spread over my body and I exhaled another long sigh. Neither woman noticed that I was even there.

"That rabble-rousing as you've been calling my work has more than paid off. The king has been doing more than just checking on the physical defenses of the city walls this past year. He's been taking the temperature of the Parlement, the church, and the people. None of them will follow him. He knows that now. You didn't see the trembling fop I saw just now. He shook every time he spoke to me. He fears me, fears the League." Montpensier's eyes began to shine and something in her demeanor reminded me of those tales my governess told me of Jeanne of Arc as a girl. Was that religious fervor I saw in them? Or increasing ambition?

"Do you really not understand how dangerous a fearful monarch can be? If the king becomes frightened enough, he will pick off Guises to take care of his problem. You are a widow and the second wife at that. You have no children to defend you, which makes it much easier for the king to send men to take you from your bed and carry you away."

Montpensier snorted, "My brothers will rescue me. If you really think I scare that easily, you know me little, Mother." If Montpensier hoped to sound defiant, she failed. She reminded me more of a petulant adolescent than a revolutionary. While she was excellent at stirring up emotion, she had few skills in leading men. It would take Henri to make a final step in revolution against the king.

❦

NOT LONG AFTER MONTPENSIER'S ESCAPE FROM ROYAL PRISON, I had my reprieve from politics, giving birth to what would be my last daughter on a chilly February morning in 1588. Unwilling to spend my last weeks of the pregnancy amidst the scheming and machinations of Paris, I left with Queen Louise for the Chateau de Blois to have my child in peace in the Loire valley. My departure also gave me a chance to escape the deteriorating relationship between Anna and Montpensier.

There were few places that felt like home as 1588 dawned: the Spanish planned to launch the Armada in May and my husband offered Normandy as a safe haven for the Spanish galleons. This defied the official word from the king, who refused to insult either his English allies or his Spanish ones. Henri Valois waited out the result of the Armada in case he backed the wrong sovereign. My husband showed no vacillation, however, and although the Duc Épernon was the new governor of Normandy and officially controlled all traffic across the region, the League promised to come to Spanish aid if needed. No matter who ruled Normandy I was not safe at Eu and could not travel there.

There was no chance of returning to Nevers, either. Since banishing me in September, Henriette refused to speak to me. Month after month, my letters went unanswered. I even resorted to writing Louis in Picardy to see if he would intervene between my sister and me, but Henriette would not see reason. The last time Henriette and I were estranged, we were fighting over money; now politics separated us. I felt isolated from my family and during my pregnancy, the timing could not have been worse.

My husband continued to refuse to return to Paris, due in part to his fear that as soon as he abandoned his troops, the king would award their command to his remaining favorite. We knew the king would make good on his threat to arrest him for seditious acts if given an opportunity. It was as if the king sensed that something was in the air, because in February, he forbade Henri from entering Paris, even to see me and our newborn daughter. Life in the field was hardly more hospitable; Épernon was Admiral of France, making it impossible for my Henri to command any French ships to come to the aid of Spanish galleons if needed. In February, the Guise returned to Nancy to decide what to do about their limited options. I did not know it at the time, but at the meeting, the Guise and Lorraine cousins made plans to assassinate Épernon and take the king hostage. Had someone had taken if Épernon care of that winter, it could have helped to reconcile my sister and I. My husband could have prevailed upon Henriette to see my side and forgive me.

I had no time to think of those things because in early February, Louise Marguerite finally came, a little past her due date. When she made her appearance, she was wrinkled and large for a newborn, but she was healthy. I was thankful that at least I had a healthy child during my time of isolation.

A week after my daughter was born, both Anna and Montpensier came to see my daughter, despite the ongoing awkwardness between the two. Anna brought gifts and congratulations from herself and from Henri's stepfather, the Duc de Nemours. Montpensier brought something besides gifts for the new child. As I sat coddling baby Louise, I noticed my sister-in-law's dress had a golden chain dangling from her belt. "Have I been so busy that I've failed to notice the current fashions? Amulets dangling from belts haven't been popular since the 1550s." I raised my eyebrows, hoping to show that I was lightly teasing her. I had no desire to incite her and have to deal with a surly sister-in-law.

Instead, she clapped her hands, "Ah, it's more than an amulet. It's a talisman!" Louise gurgled, and I turned to check that she was not choking. When I returned my attention to Montpensier, she was holding a small pair of golden scissors. I frowned, unable to imagine what she could need a pair of scissors for.

"It's for the king. I am preparing him for his third crown." The tone of her voice made me hesitate. I knew that I did not want her to elaborate, so I tried to change the subject. She refused to be swayed, however, and continued to speak, her hands jabbing at the air while she spoke.

"He has two crowns, one of Poland and one of France. He is so devoted to his church I think he needs a third crown on his royal head —that of a tonsure." She smiled triumphantly.

I had heard nothing of the king joining a religious order. True, he had taken part in extreme religious activities since taking the throne in 1574. Many of his confidants followed him in religious processions where they self-flagellated. I had heard him speak of spending time at a monastery in the spring when the ice melted, and the weather was milder. Queen Louise was also extremely devout, but neither of them had spoken of their desire to retire to a monastic life.

I opened my mouth to speak, but Montpensier cut me off. "The king will need to shave his head when he enters religious life. No one would want to defile the body of the king by killing him. We will remove him from his throne and sent to live out his life in quiet contemplation. It's perfect for a scholar like him. He's not meant to govern, only to feed his soul. Don't you see? It's the perfect solution for France!"

"Is that what they decided in Nancy?" Henri was guarded in his news of the decisions made in Nancy. He knew that the health of our child distracted me too much to even bother with external politics. Now, with a child on my knee, I was no longer saddled with the phys- ical demands of pregnancy. If I wished to take an active part in the League's activities, I could afford to leave Louise in the care of a nurse and devote my time to promoting the League in Paris. The thought was appealing. I had resented the feeling of being sidelined while events swirled around me. I was also nearing thirty and would be at the end of my childbearing days.

She shrugged. "The king is inept, and we should place him where he can do good. France would be stronger with a Regent popular with the nobles and with the people."

I lifted my eyebrows, intrigued. "Henri would serve as regent? But who would become king? France cannot be ruled by a Regent for long."

She cocked her head to the side. "Well, we Guise are descendants of the Capets. We have royal blood in our veins. The Valois came to the throne when there was no other option available."

"But by law, Navarre is the heir to the throne."

She shook her head, "The Pope has already issued a bull of Excommunication. Navarre can not take the throne. Without the Vatican to support him, he will never be king."

That meant that my eldest son would be the heir to the throne. I would become Queen Mother. The idea immediately appealed. "Tell me more."

"Well, Henri has promised to give the king a distraction in May when the Armada sails. The king will be too busy with this 'distraction' to worry about the Spanish."

I lifted my eyebrows, completely seduced. "Tell me more about this 'distraction'."

⚜

By Spring, Montpensier and I were working in tandem to head the Parisian Leaguers, she taking the role of the public face of discontent, while in public, I wrung my hands in the king's presence and wailed about my inability to reign in my excitable sister-in-law. My husband and I exchanged letters, with him promising me that Spain would send three-hundred-thousand ecus to fund a revolt against the king in May. We had only to fan the flames of discontent until then.

I opened the doors of the Hotel de Guise to any English emigres looking for sanctuary and for onlookers to see the strength of the international Catholic cause. "Monsieur," I nodded at Nicolas Poulain, one of the most dedicated members of the League in the city. He had spent the past three years supervising the surreptitious movement of weapons to the hotel and safe houses across the city. He had just returned from the countryside, where he encouraged supporters across Paris to do the same thing.

"Madame la Duchesse," he nodded at me and I noticed that he had a thick pamphlet in his hand. "I wonder if you've had a look at this. It's fresh off the printing blocks."

Entitled, "The Tragic and Remarkable Story of Piers Gaveston," the pamphlet told in both English and French the story of the English king and his perverse relationship with his male lover. "I suppose our English brethren are familiar with the story, no?"

He nodded, "And now, the French will know about it. Even the basest peasant will know what happens to a king who commits sodomy and consorts with rabble." I had heard whispers of the king engaging in sexual relations with his favorites, but I had witnessed nothing inappropriate between them. From the moment he married Louise, he took pains to remain faithful to her. The rumors seemed more like spite, but sodomy was a serious charge for a faithful Catholic. It would be enough to excommunicate the king and turn his subjects against him. A pang of guilt rose in me. I knew the king was likely innocent, but by that point, I had gone too far in my own rebellions against him.

"Sir," a page came up to Poulain, a note in his hand. "Madame, I'm afraid I have some bad news." He read the missive, his face growing dark. "I'm afraid that the king's troops have taken over several villages in Picardy from Aumale. It forced him to fall back into the countryside."

I held my hand up to my throat. This was a huge loss for the League. With no promise from Épernon and the king, the Spanish ships had only the League's guarantee of a safe port. Even worse, if the Armada were to fail, the English troops might come spilling over French soil, starting with the Boulogne that we had lost months earlier.

"Not to worry, My Lady. I'm sure they can fix it. If you'll excuse me." He bowed and strode away from me. Moments later, Montpensier was at my side. "We're losing more villages to the Protestants." She gasped and at the sound, my shoulders sank. They shrank further when I looked up to see Mendoza stalking towards us.

"Madame, soon your husband's forces cannot hold any location they guaranteed us. King Philip has risked so much for the Guise cause, I would think one section of the country would be no problem. Even a small seaport was too much for them."

"I think you've underestimated the determination of French forces, Señor," I snapped at him so quickly that it shocked even Montpensier.

Well, let her be; she was not the only firebrand in the family. I would play second to her for no longer.

"Phillip has had my county of Eu at his disposal for months. If it is not enough, then I question the might of the Spanish fleet. Is Phillip so unsure of his victory over the English he needs a guarantee from France?" Henri would berate me for baiting the Spanish ambassador later, but my temper was up, and I wanted to take my anger out on someone, preferably someone who challenged my family.

Instead of retreating in shame, Mendoza instead stepped close to my ear. "Be careful, My Lady; kings do not take kindly to treason and you and your family are at the forefront of just such activity."

"We are standing for France, for her strength and her future. If Spain is so strong, then I wonder why you spend so much time skulking around our country looking for friends? From my perspective, Phillip looks to be weak."

"You will regret those words come this summer, My Lady. Oh, and I'd advise you to get rid of that traitor you're welcoming into your house." Throwing on his cloak, he left the room without so much as asking my leave. Fine, I was more than glad to be rid of him. Beside me, Montpensier exhaled loudly. I blinked; I had forgotten all about her presence. "I'd forgotten how terrifying you can be when angry, Sister."

Mendoza's mention of a traitor unnerved me. There were untold numbers of men moving in and out of the Hotel de Guise. How was I to know who was loyal to us and who was using our hospitality as a ruse?

FOR THE NEXT TWO WEEKS, EVERY PERSON WHO WALKED INTO MY home was suspect. Every note I sent to Joinville went under coded message. When I spoke to my husband, it was only to talk of our children, including Louise who grew more robust by the day. In my paranoia, I hired and dismissed servants at will, including ones who had served the Guise family for years.

Unable to discover the false friend in our midst, I started to lose hope. Looking back, I should not have lost hope so easily. On April 11th, fifteen members of the sixteen came to my home, caps in hand.

"Poulain has betrayed us." One man ran his hand through his hair, the wrinkles in his face deepening as he spoke. "We've been strengthening our militia, to prepare for May. We knew that the king had stationed men in each quarter as spies. We were arrogant enough to think we'd identified all of them." He turned to the others, raising his hand in surrender. "We missed one, the biggest traitor of all."

I sighed, the words I'd said to Mendoza within Poulain's earshot reverberating in my ears. Enough words to damn me. Enough words to put me on a scaffold if Henri Valois wished to do so. "Was he always on the king's payroll? Or did he turn his coat these last few days?"

Another spoke up. "We don't know for sure. All we do know is that the first chance he got, he slipped away and ran to the Louvre to warn the king that we were arming. We have to tell the Duc that the king knows of our plans. He has to come to Paris to rescue us."

"But, how can he come now? The king will be waiting for him." Even more dangerous were the spring storms, which would make the roads between Nancy and Paris a quagmire. One determined man on a single horse could make it to Paris, but not the leagues of men Henri would need to confront the king.

"He must come. It's likely that the king will pick off Guise allies to break his power. We've got to depose the king and do it as soon as possible. To do it properly, we'll need your husband in Paris."

Two weeks later, his words came true. Seeing the Duc d'Elbeuf as the most vulnerable Leaguer, the king sent the bulk of French forces were not under my husband's control into Rouen. This time, however, the king overextended his forces. With his own army in faraway Normandy, he left the capital open to invasion. Days after the army marched westwards to Normandy, I received a triumphant letter from Nancy. After two years away, my husband was finally coming back to Paris and back to his family.

❦   6   ❦

As a girl, I used to scoff at stories of women who lingered at home, waiting for their men to come home. I thought those women weak and passive, merely sitting by as the world passed them. I suppose after months apart, I could be forgiven for my excitement on May 9th when a messenger came running in, crying that the Duc de Guise had finally returned to Paris.

While Henri made his triumphant return to the city that loved him, a crowd swelled around his horse. Crying, "Long live the Guise—the pillar of the church!" they proclaimed their loyalty to our family. As we had hoped, we had the loyalty of the populace firmly on our side. As the news spread, the hotel turned into a hive of activity. Months of speculation and weeks of preparation were finally a reality. Like a romantic ninny, I stood at the top of the great steps of the second floor of the hotel, waiting to see my husband. A part of me held out the hope he would stride into the hotel, laughing at his victory over the king.

After half an hour of standing and waiting for my husband to wander into our home, a small figure appeared in the doorway. Seeing it was Montpensier, I felt bitter disappointment she arrived before her brother. "He's gone to the Louvre," she announced as she took off her cloak.

"Already? Is he gone to depose the king then?" I frowned; the pace of this uprising was much faster than I had expected.

"He's with the Queen Mother. He figured it would be safe to claim he was here at her behest. Even with no army, Henri Valois can be slippery as an eel. Guise figured that if he put out the word, he wanted to make amends with the king, he could walk into the Louvre without so much as a shot being fired."

"And how did he get Catherine de Medici to go with him?" My husband had a silver tongue but convincing the king's mother to accompany him on his way to depose the king took incredible skill.

"She's going in her litter and he's walking beside her. It's so gallant! He's keeping the angry crowds off the old woman." That was wise, given the crowd's growing dislike of the Queen Mother. Without their golden champion to tone down their emotions, they might tear the diminutive Catherine de Medici to shreds.

I called for food and with Montpensier sitting beside me in my salon; I learned the events of the day as they unfolded. I soon realized that I would not see my husband until nightfall, or even later. As he and the Queen Mother slowly made their way towards the Louvre with a crowd of thousands, news reached the king and his council that the Duc de Guise had defied royal decree and entered Paris. "Henri Valois was furious! He stood there with his Privy Council debating what to do next. They were just like a bunch of boys, pissing themselves at hearing the lord of the manor had returned. They took so long debating on what to do, that my brother was at the door of the council chamber before they could decide. So, there he walked in, with Catherine de Medici as his escort."

She dissolved into giggles. I could only imagine the awkwardness of the occasion. Still, knowing the king's paranoia, I knew that my husband was in danger, the Queen Mother's presence notwithstanding. Playing for the time, the king drew my husband into Queen Louise's chamber, a place I would normally be, but on that day, I had begged leave to attend to personal business. "My brother told the king that the present estrangement between them was because of Épernon. He's determined to make it clear to the king that everything is because of the favorites, not a quarrel he has with the king."

"Did the king take the bait?" I knew that he would not, but I had to know how the king took this latest ruse. My husband had marched confidently into the Louvre itself and now, had to talk his way out of there alive.

"No, he quoted the saying that 'he who loves the master should love his dog.'" At that, I rolled my eyes. If the king had not surrounded himself with such common mutts, no one would have reason to love them.

"How did Henri answer him?"

"He responded, 'Provided he does not bite.'" I snorted at that; it sounded like him.

"So, now where are they?" I glanced around, noting that the evening sun was slanting in the windows.

"Henri will do his duty as Grand Master of France, presiding over a supper at the Louvre."

I rolled my eyes, "I suppose that means I won't see my husband until Midnight?"

I DID NOT SEE MY HUSBAND UNTIL WELL PAST MIDNIGHT. Following him, dozens of retainers flooded into the courtyard of the Hotel de Guise and I spent the long hours getting provisions set up for the extra mouths I was to feed. My Henri stayed close to the king and the Queen Mother for hours, knowing that if he was beside them, they could hardly withdraw to plot against him.

Flushed with exhaustion, I finally heard the thump of my husband's boots as he came into the house. "Henri!" I shouted, taking the two stories of grand stairs as I rushed towards him like a lovesick young girl. Embracing him, I noticed a tear in the linen of his shirt. "Are you injured? What happened?"

He glanced down and grabbed at his right forearm. "Ah, it's nothing. A woman pulled at my sleeve and she refused to let go. I suppose this shirt is a little old." He looked at me and gave me a shrug.

"It's unseemly. Here, come with me." I pulled him behind me and marched into my bedchamber. Once inside, I tugged his shirt off and carefully inspected him for wounds. "Well, I suppose you are all right."

"See, I told you I was fine." He gave me a sunny smile, one completely out of place with the situation at hand. To my shame, that smile melted my heart and my long months of missing my husband rose to mock me. I was too weak to resist, and we spent the night in one another's arms.

❧

THE NEXT MORNING, MY HUSBAND ROSE TO DRESS FOR MASS. "I promised the king I would attend with him. All of Paris will be watching." I knew that it was only an outward show, meant to cool down the fevered pitch the city had risen to the day before. If I had any common sense, I would have stayed at home. Naturally, I had no common sense, and I decided I must accompany him.

"I am a lady-in-waiting to the queen, it would be best if I sat with the two of you." Unwilling to start an argument, he shrugged his shoulder in agreement. Bundled into the Guise coach, we made our way through the crowded streets to the church for the service.

Flushed with the wave of emotion we felt at his return, I basked in the adulation in the church. Hundreds of curious onlookers came to the church to see the king and Guise reconcile before the Host. Reveling in my position as the wife of the triumphant Duc, I became too overconfident that morning.

During Mass, I looked at the assembled crowd to find an unwelcome blonde head amongst the worshippers. Charlotte de Sauve was in the congregation. I hadn't seen the woman since Christmas and something convinced me I had seen the last of her. Had she been in Paris the entire time, or did she trail behind my husband like a camp follower? Where had that damned woman been the entire time? My mind raced with explanations as the Mass droned on. My anger gnawed at me, fueling my apprehension minute by minute. Her presence was an offense, and it spoiled the triumph I felt in having my husband returned to me.

I wanted to go to her, to snatch the pious lace veil from her head. I fantasized about grabbing her by the hair and pulling her out of the church, exposing her as a spy and a traitor. I would learn that day who she was working for, why she was so determined to attach herself to my husband. She reminded me that no matter how many victories the League earned, there would always be those in the shadows, acting for unknown agents. She was danger incarnate.

Once Mass was over, I rose to confront her, the consequences for my husband be damned. Before I could do so, Henri took my arm and guided me towards the king. "Henri, I need to speak to you about that woman." I glanced to see her retreating shoulders as she moved steadily away from me. I would not have a confrontation with Charlotte de Sauve. At the door, her current husband, the Marquise de Noirmoutier, took her forearm and whispered in her ear.

"Not now, the king is waiting." He pulled me towards the king's party and away from my perch spying on the woman warming my husband's bed. A churlish feeling of rebellion swept over me.

"I see the entire Privy Council is here." Noirmoutier was amongst the few men the king added halfheartedly in response to the allegations that his favorites had taken over the upper echelons of power in France. I wondered if the man was a cuckold or if he was complicit in his wife's infidelity. Many men used a comely wife as a weapon to climb further up the social ladder. Was he playing both sides, sending his wife to Henri's bed? If that were the case, she was even more dangerous than I had feared. She could prove to be more dangerous than the traitor Poulain.

"Are you really so stupid as to be consorting with that woman here in Paris?" After he had spent the night in my arms, no less. Jealousy tinged with anger rose within me. As I seethed, Henri turned to accept the welcomes from well-wishers. His determination to ignore me and play the politician further stoked my anger.

"Catherine, now is not the time to indulge in jealousy. We'll talk about this later." Once again, he was sweeping away my fear for his safety, labeling it as jealousy of a woman scorned. I couldn't take any more of his behavior, so I turned and stalked out of the church. On the carriage ride home, I fumed at the thick-headed husband they had cursed me with. He might have all of Paris at his feet, but he remained blind to the dangers wrapping their perfumed white limbs about him as he slept.

As I climbed out of my carriage, I noticed a young officer shouting directions to the surrounding men. "Madame," he tipped his hat, and I nodded in response. "Not to worry, Paris is safe in Guise hands. The city is not in danger of invasion."

I frowned, "Why on earth would it be in danger?" I had heard nothing of a danger of invasion.

"Well, the city has the sacred right to arm itself. By law, the king cannot send troops in to quell an uprising. We're safe from any reprisals from the king." His last words chilled me. Was there a danger of Henri Valois taking his revenge on my husband for coming to Paris in defiance of his order? Would he send in troops, despite the city's traditional rights? There were many royal troops embedded in the League troops across the city. I glanced around and tried to see if I could detect a traitor before my eyes. Alas, like Poulain, I could not guess which might be a Judas amongst us.

"Madame la Guise, are you all right? I'm sorry to have scared you. We really are safe behind the walls of the Hotel de Guise." I felt safe behind the walls of the three-story complex, which since January, had become less a home and more of a fortress. They quartered men amongst the stables and outbuildings, and I even heard rumors that some of the youngest amongst them were sleeping in our Orangerie. I craned my neck and peered towards it, vowing to check in on the boys, who were no older than my eldest son.

"Besides, with Condé gone, the Protestants are no threat to us." At that, my head jerked up. "What? What happened to Condé? Did he go back to England?"

He shuffled his feet and looked around for someone to pass me onto regretting his decision to talk. "Word just came through—the Prince de Condé died at the hands of his wife."

The ground spun beneath me. Once, Condé's wife was my sister, Marie. He had married his second, wealthy wife less than two years earlier. So, the wife he had shut up in a golden cage had relieved him of his earthly burden? I had to laugh at the irony. Our irascible brother-in-law was gone. Seconds later, I realized that this meant my niece Catherine was now officially an orphan. Although she had never met the garlic-faced man, the news would pain her. I strode into the main house and into my chambers. As soon as I could, I would write to Catherine and give her my sympathies.

❦

HENRI DID NOT COME TO MY BED THAT NIGHT. I DO NOT KNOW where he spent the night, although I suspect it was in some home used by Charlotte de Sauve. I went to bed that night furious with my husband and resolved to seek him out in the morning to confront his lackadaisical attitude towards his latest mistress.

My mind was reeling as I rose that morning, but I wanted to do my duty towards my family before I confronted the situation with Madame de Sauve. At six that morning, I sat down to write a letter to Catherine, reassuring her of our love as her true parents. Although she was now of an age to be betrothed, I avoided the topic to respect her time of mourning for the father who had abandoned her before her birth. Once I finished the letter and posted it to Joinville, I sent a second letter to Henriette, telling her of my plans for our niece. Hopefully, she would put aside her anger towards me and answer this letter for the sake of young Marie.

Just before eight, I heard a commotion in the courtyard below. This was nothing new since additional troops had been quartering in our home and the surrounding buildings of our section of Paris for weeks. Thinking it was a drill, I turned back to my letter,

The door opened with a crash and I looked up to see my lady's maid, Suzanne, her face ashen. "Madame, the king!"

"What, he's here?" I blinked, unable to understand what had her so upset. "Why would the king come here?"

She wrung her hands, "No, he's ordered troops into Paris! We're being attacked by the royal army. The king has sent his troops out against the people of Paris!" She grew more hysterical with each word and by the time she stopped speaking, I could barely understand her. Coming to my feet, I decided to seek out my husband and see what was going on.

I found him leaning over a large map of the city, men hanging onto him like a nest of ants. He seemed calm, which told me that there was no reason to panic. Until he took to his own horse and unsheathed his own sword, there was no danger. "What is going on?"

He looked up at me and expelled a long sigh. "The king brought in troops, including some of his Swiss mercenaries. They've been sneaking into every street of the city since before daybreak."

"Then, we really are being invaded? The king violated the city's right to be free of troops?" Henri Valois continued to indiscriminately violate every civil liberty that his subjects enjoyed. I rubbed my mouth with my hand. This was what a panicked king could do when cornered. "What are you going to do?"

The men looked at me, unused to hearing such questions from a woman. "Stay here by all means. Where the invaders are, there is little resistance. It caught too many people unaware and unable to put up a defense. There is no telling how many women and children are vulnerable to these villains." He crossed himself and the rest hurriedly did the same.

"What about the ones who *could* defend themselves?" I would ask before it hung longer in the air between us.

"The troops we could station can hold off the invaders. We have loyal men across the city, so we can hold our positions there." Henri straightened and cleared his throat, a typical signal he was busy with other matters and could bother no longer to explain things to his wife. None of them bothered to mention that many of those men stationed by the man who had given up the plot to the king and betrayed us all. A sudden fear struck me, could Poulain be in league with Charlotte de Sauve? Was that why the strumpet was back in Paris?

"As there will be many innocent victims of the king's betrayal, I think I should organize relief efforts." My husband gave me a curt nod of dismissal and I nodded in reply. In the hallway, my Suzanne met me. "Madame, my son is young, I should be with him."

I did not want to send her out into the street with little to defend herself, but before I could protest, she pulled a knife from her skirts. "My husband is loyal to the Duc and to the League. Once I get to our home, we will barricade ourselves in and defend our home. I cannot do that here." Her eyes pleaded with me and I knew that I could not refuse her. She was only a few years younger than I and it terrified me at what she could face once she left the safety of the hotel. Still, there was no way I could stop her from leaving.

"Go, but be careful as you go." I turned to the rest of the staff and commandeered any space in the hotel not used by my husband's men for relief efforts. We compiled any supplies we could find, bandages for injuries, blankets and all the food we could spare. The last item was scarce since it stretched us thin feeding the men billeted within the hotel. I sorely missed having Montpensier at my side. Marshaling relief efforts was exactly what she could manage, but her hotel was outside the city walls, within the faubourgs that encircled Paris. I could not risk the lives of my pages to get a message to her. I would have to wait until the League troops surrounded and disarmed the invading troops.

I continued my work until just after noon, using my vantage point just outside of the study to monitor my husband's activities. Suddenly, my husband marched out of the study on his way out of the front door. Running after him, I caught up with him at the steps to the ground floor. "Where are you possibly going?"

"I will address my men," he spat, impatience straining his voice. "The king has ordered me to leave the city at once."

"Are you actually going to play the coward and leave?"

He laughed, a deep sound that echoed across the courtyard. "Hardly. I've been sending messages to the king and to my troops. Only I can negotiate a cease-fire between these invaders and my troops. If the king wants to avoid a massacre, he needs me to stay in Paris."

"How benevolent of you, to create a conflict and emerge as the man to end it." He smirked at me enjoying his role as peacemaker. "I have to go now, wife. Stay inside," he held up a single finger, bidding me to stay rooted at the spot as if I were a hunting dog he was training. With that, my husband walked out of the courtyard like a madman, waving and doffing his hat as the crowd roared their approval. For most of that afternoon, he paraded down street after street of League held areas, basking in the peoples' adoration. I could only shake my head and wonder if my husband had taken leave of his senses.

His overconfidence was a folly, of that I was certain. Catherine de Medici had weathered enough riots and uprisings in the middle of Paris and this one would be no different. She had trekked to the Louvre at my husband's side out of necessity, but given the slightest opportunity, she would turn the situation around to her beloved son's advantage. As the afternoon wore on, the king's troops proved to little more than fodder for the populace. Citizens raised makeshift block-ades to trap the men in the streets of the city, streets that the foreigners and Frenchmen from across the country did not know of. Once trapped, they easily picked them off as the people fired at them from balconies and windows. By sunset, there were dead soldiers lying in every street in Paris. The king had risen against his people and his people responded by rising against him.

LATE THAT AFTERNOON, THE HOTEL ONCE AGAIN WAS ABLAZE WITH the word that we were about to receive a royal visitor, the Queen Mother herself. This was hardly a social occasion but, befitting her status as the king's most respected negotiator, we had to scurry to prepare the hotel for her visit. While I supervised the domestic aspects of the visit, Henri rushed around to prepare himself. The two would meet in private, with no other visitors in the room. I placed my hand on my husband's forearm and looked into his eyes. "What are you going to ask of her?'

He pursed his lips, "I want the king to do more than just dismiss Épernon. They must banish him and the rest of the favorites from court. I want those brigands, his Forty-Five disbanded. What kind of coward needs a personal guard? He is not the Emperor of Rome. And," he held up his pointer finger, "He must immediately ban Navarre from the succession."

I folded my arms, "Do you really think she will agree to that?"

"We hold Paris at this moment. She has no cards left to play. Or, rather, her son has no cards to play. We have finally won Paris for the Church."

"If she agrees to bar Navarre's succession, are you going to put forth Cardinal de Bourbon as the heir?" My uncle was too old to marry and produce an heir, we all knew that. Louis XII had in his desperation married Mary Tudor to produce a male heir, but he died within months of the marriage. The next in line would be our eldest son or the eldest son of the Duc de Lorraine. Either son would put our cause on the throne, but I would prefer my Charles to become king.

"Yes. If I show that I'm solidly behind Bourbon, they 'll see me as promoting a man of the church, not my family. Neither of us can predict when your uncle will meet his Lord." He smirked at the thought.

"Navarre could still come to the king's aid. He can't waste time in the countryside, whoring around and mourning Condé's death forever."

"That is another reason I need to have the king agree to my terms as soon as possible." Before he could finish, he jerked his head up, indicating that the Queen Mother was in the courtyard. The woman who walked through our door looked like a gaunt version of her former self. Gout had sapped most of her energy and she looked a pitiable shade of gray. "Madame," I sank to my knees in reverence.

"Madame de Guise, it would seem that we are at a dark day for France. Here I am, speaking for my son's throne."

"I believe that we are all speaking for the French throne. My husband only wants to remove the bumpkins who have infiltrated--" she cut me off with an upward tilt of her head. I curtseyed, looking my husband in the eye as I did so.

The two spent the better part of three hours negotiating, with the sounds of their voices carrying far outside of the study walls. At last, we heard "I will carry your terms to His Majesty," and we scurried from our listening perches before the door opened. A few moments later, Catherine de Medici swooped out of the door and made her slow, torturous way back to the Louvre.

"THAT DAMNED FOOL!" MY HUSBAND BURST INTO THE DINING ROOM early the next morning as I was quietly having breakfast with Montpensier. His face was flush with blood as he entered, a sure sign he was on one of his emotional rampages. To calm him, I delicately placed my fork on my plate and looked up at him, hands folded in my lap.

"Dearest, what is it now? Is it Mayenne?" The two brothers had been at odds for months, arguing on tactics for dealing with the Swiss mercenaries in the field. Hopefully, it was just another fraternal argument.

He placed his hands on the chair next to Montpensier, his knuckles turning white. "No, it is the king. He fled the city last night and we still don't know where he plans to go."

"Perhaps to a monastery." Montpensier could not hide a smirk as she piped up beside him.

"I couldn't be that lucky. It's likely that while I was squandering my time 'negotiating' with his Mother, the king was busy planning his escape."

The story poured out of him, as his anger rose. Yesterday, the Queen Mother had invited my husband to meet with her again at the Louvre, where she would give him the king's response. Before Catherine could leave her rooms at her own hotel, word had already leaked out that the king left on a stroll at the nearby Tuileries and slipped out a side door to freedom.

"Both of they had duped me. The damned Valois, they're slippery as eels! Where I to--" a page whispered in his ear, breaking his mood for a moment. "Really? Here? Ha—then, by all means, send her in!"

Before I could ask him what was going on, Catherine de Medici appeared in the doorway of our dining room. We rose to our feet and curtsied, never forgetting our stations. Henri, so battle-hardened by years in the field and in the royal court, recovered far faster than either of us women could.

"Madame, you have deceived me. While you have kept me talking, the king has left Paris and gone where he can stir up more trouble for me."

Her face blanched even further. Never had I seen anyone give Catherine de Medici such a dressing down. If she were she anyone else,

I would think her a vulnerable old woman, too fragile to endure this verbal assault

"My son told me none of this. I swear to you, I went to the Louvre and presented your demands to him, as you asked. He said he would need time to consider them. He promised me, his mother, that he would give an answer today. He never hinted that he would do something so cowardly."

Her voice shook as she spoke. She looked bewildered. For a woman who spent most of her adult life outmaneuvering and always staying two steps ahead of everyone, she looked very much out of her league. And afraid. Even my husband must have sensed her fear because he softened his tone towards her for the rest of their short conversation.

THE NEWS THAT THE KING HAD FLED PARIS IN DISGRACE, PROVED TO be all too true and that news spread across Paris like wildfire. The few men left of the invaders the king called into the city, quickly disbanded and fled towards the countryside. With no need to defend themselves, the populace removed the barricades, and the city became Guise territory. Within three days, my husband and his allies in the Sixteen commanded all the main fortifications of the city: the Arsenal, the Bastille, and the chateau of Vincennes. There were no troops in Paris loyal to the king left to defend his reign.

In the absence of a royal government, Paris made its own government under the guidance of the Sixteen and my husband. They would base offices of every level on merit, not through bribery and nepotism. The king had violated the city's civil liberties and with him gone the people were eager to restore them.

On the sixteenth of May, Montpensier could no longer contain her glee over the king's withdrawal. Taking advantage of a newly abandoned Hotel de Ville, she threw open the building's doors for a victory celebration. She packed the salon with bodies, including several Spaniards. Chief amongst them was Mendoza himself, who could not keep himself from bragging about this present to the King of Spain.

"Madame de Guise, France has given Spain perfect peace. Our

Armada will sail to England on her Holy mission with no impediments. I owe your husband my thanks." He raised his glass in a toast and unwilling to get into a debate with him, I raised mine. Judging from his appearance, he was three glasses of brandy into the night already.

"I hope this demonstration proves to Phillip that France is more than capable of defending her borders and the Holy Church." Unlike me, Montpensier had no qualms about provoking the might of Spain. Also, unlike me, she had no children to worry about if our relationship with Spain took an ugly turn. Luckily, Mendoza ambled off to receive more congratulations and more drink.

"Isn't it a little reckless to be taunting Spain like that? By autumn, they'll be ruling England and knocking at two of our borders." I hissed in her ear, as she took a sip of her wine.

"You' doing not see the larger picture. Now they have humiliated the king, the Estates-General will rule France. That means it will unite us nobles, instead of marginalized. We will go from a weak king to a strong rule by the nobles. Plus," she took a pastry from a proffered tray, "my brothers control our military. If Spain were foolhardy to attempt an attack, they will cut them down on the battlefield."

She was blind to her overconfidence, but once again, I held my tongue. As much as I prayed she was right, I still had my doubts that the king was truly brought to heel. As that thought filtered through my mind, I looked up to see the diminutive figure of Catherine de Medici enter the room.

All conversations stopped. She was no stranger to hostile gatherings, but this evening, things were different. Her son had been all but deposed. It shocked me that she would appear at such a gathering, yet there she stood, right in front of us swathed in black mourning garb like a crow. She stood for a moment, stock still. Seconds later, the pain from her gout returned, and she called for a seat. Acting the solicitous hostess, Montpensier called two servants in to bring the Queen Mother of France her chair.

She settled down in her chair, all eyes upon her. Eventually, the musicians returned to their songs and conversations resumed in the hall. In a silent battle for territory, Montpensier refused to withdraw from the Queen Mother, earning her older woman's irritation.

"Catherine of Lorraine, do you really think it's proper to hold a fete when the city is in such a turmoil?" The Queen Mother arched an eyebrow and turned to glare at Montpensier. The Matrons in her royal entourage turned to stare at my sister-in-law in curiosity.

Montpensier burst into laughter, the high sound resounding like a dinner bell, "What would you have me do, Madame? I am like a brave soldier with a heart swollen with victory! We have driven the Swiss invaders back and Paris is safe!" She threw out her hands in a melodramatic gesture. Beside her, the Queen Mother "harrumphed!" in disgust, saying nothing more. An awkward silence followed, with Montpensier, for once, failing to find the words for a comeback. As much as I wanted to see the rest of their showdown, a tug at my elbow held my attention.

I turned to see my maid, Suzanne, who I had hadn't seen in four days, beaming up at me. "I'm sorry, Madame—I could not get back to you earlier. There was a small company of Swiss held up in my brother's home. We've been hiding from them until the men loyal to the Guise could free us." They had opened the gathering to all levels of society, with jubilant nobles rubbing shoulders with the lower classes. The entire city belonged to the Guise, and we would celebrate that fact with all of them.

❦ 7 ❦

The next two months filled with moves and countermoves between the Guise cause and a divided Valois household. Paris remained solidly declared for the Guise and the Catholic League. Catherine de Medici spent the Summer in Paris, going to the Hotel de Guise so often that she soon became a fixture at our dinner table. The King continued to cower in fear, holding out in the city of Chartres. In his absence, his bewildered mother did all that she could to hold the government of France together.

We continued to celebrate the liberation of Paris and her people from the foreign Invaders, with the people flocking to our banner. Less than two months after the day of liberation, which the people later called the Day of the Barricades, I learned that I was once again pregnant. A child is a particular blessing, and I have loved all of my children dearly but learning I would be with child for the fourteenth time made me despair. I had harbored a secret hope I would be past my childbearing years and to learn that there was another baby growing inside me, made me quite upset.

Henri was quite pleased. My Henri ways always good with people.

He had a particular touch with children, whether they were his own or not. My news delighted him, "Ah, so I see we celebrated more than we realized when the king fled." I did not find his jest particularly amusing. By my own calculations, I would give birth for the second time during the chilliest part of Winter, most likely in February. My youngest, Marie-Louise was barely walking, her older sister Jeanne not much older and I would have another child in the nursery.

In August, Henri saddled his horse and left south for Chartres to parley with the king to make provisions for a convention of the Estates-General. Riding alongside him were eighty well-armed men, the Cardinal of Bourbon, fifty archers and my Mother-in-law, the Dowager Duchesse de Guise, and the Dowager Duchesse de Nemours. "It's best you and the child remain back in Paris where it's safe," Henri warned me. He was right: outside of the walls of Paris, the king still ruled France and we were at risk.

They accomplished little during those talks. While outwardly, he and the king displayed every pleasantry, their rivalry still simmered just beneath the surface. A few days after Henri's party arrived at Chartres, Bernardino Mendoza virtually danced into the cathedral of Chartres and announced to the Guise party that the Armada had cut the English navy to pieces. For a few moments, it seemed as if everything we had worked for had come true. A Spanish victory would cut the heart of English Protestants and their supplies to the French. Less than an hour later, the king appeared and informed Mendoza that he had left Paris without hearing the whole report of the Armada. The king had heard the terrible news that had been sweeping across northern France that day; the mighty Armada of Spain lay at the bottom of the English Channel. Now the way from England to Calais lay unchecked and vulnerable. Henri's invincible patron had finally suffered a devastating blow.

❧

It was unseasonably warm in the Salle d'Estate of the Chateau de Blois. One might expect October to give us a break from the relentless heat of the past Summer, but we were not so lucky. It was if the cavernous room echoed the king's fury in being called to hold a representative meeting packed with men who opposed him. The buzz of barely concealed contempt competed with the humidity, making it a miserable afternoon for us all. My condition excluded me in the meetings in Chartres, but I could not miss a meeting of the Estates-General. I had not seen Henri since Chartres, as he took every opportunity to return to the king's side when not out in the provinces. The king even extended his courtesy towards Montpensier, insisting that the Guise woman occupy the best rooms at Blois.

The ladies of the court packed the gallery facing the throne. Not since the days of the king's grandfather, the jovial Francis I had the court seen so many glittering ladies assembled in a single place. Facing beside her husband, Queen Louise looked pale and withdrawn, the only Guise woman who did not share in our triumph. Fifteen years of balancing her family's disdain for her husband and her spouse's erratic behavior had finally worn her down. My heart went out to her. Her sister, Marguerite, widow of the Duc de Joyeuse, sat with her, clothed in black and constantly weeping for her husband. The two spent most of their waking hours in prayer.

More upsetting was the absence of my sister, Henriette. Although due to arrive in October with the rest of the court ladies, she had made one excuse after another to delay coming to court, to avoid seeing me. A year after banishing me from her home, she had still not forgiven me. I had all but given up hope she ever would.

Taking his place as Grand Master of the Court, Henri had finally realized his dream of recognition as was his due as a Prince of Lorraine. Finally, the years of working to remove the king's dandies and unworthy men looked to be over and they restored the Houses of Lorraine and Guise to their place in the governing of France. Joyeuse was dead and Épernon neutralized, the king suddenly seeing reason had dismissed his former ministers. Relief spread over our faction. I stood at the women's gallery of Blois, fighting nausea, but still flushed with pride for my husband. Henri's place was in front of the king, the traditional seat of the Lord High Steward. Yet, placed as he was, in front of the king and with his back turned towards the beleaguered monarch, the symbolism of their placement lost on no one in attendance that sweltering day in October. He preceded Henri Valois in the assembly and in the hearts of the French people.

Rising, the king addressed the assembly in eloquent words and I held my breath as I watched Henri's face to see his reactions. Stating his continued devotion to the mission of the Holy Church, he continued for several moments to extol the Queen Mother and her skills in negotiation. I looked over at Catherine de Medici, who looked old and frail. Her granddaughter Christine, a Lorraine princess, would marry a Medici in two months' time and the Estates-General session at Blois was in part to celebrate their nuptials. Suffused with the heat and finding my fan incapable of keeping me cool, I drifted off as the king continued his speech.

Suddenly, his tone changed. "Some of the greatest princes of my realm have entered unlawful leagues and associations; but in the exercise of my accustomed clemency, I desire to obliterate the memory of the past; and to relieve the natural fear which assails many of my loving subjects, that after my demise they may fall under the dominion of a heretic prince, I have caused this august assembly to be convoked to remedy this evil and to restore order, justice, and submission to the laws throughout my kingdom." I glanced over again at Henri, who remained as still as a statue.

Would the king attempt to punish the League for treason despite his speech of reconciliation? His words were a direct attack on my husband, yet the king knew he held no cards. They packed the Estates-General with League adherents, with little to no men allied to the king. Henri had been part of the game for too long to panic at the slightest hint of danger. Nor was he gullible enough to fall for honeyed-words spoken to a room full of nobles. As my mind raced with possibilities, the king stated that he would accept the demands of the League.

I FOUND MY HUSBAND AT THE DOOR OF THE CARDINAL DE Bourbon's lodgings. Pleading an indisposition, the Cardinal had missed the opening session and had not heard the king's speech. "Henri," I clutched his doublet in terror.

"Come," he pulled me into the Cardinal's antechamber. Glancing over his shoulder to see that no one was watching at the door, he shut the portal and ushered us well inside the room before he spoke. Before he could, a knock sounded, and he opened the door to admit the Cardinal de Lyon and his younger brother, the Cardinal de Guise. Fastening the door behind him, his brother hastened to the middle of the room with us.

"The king has inferred that we are traitors, Gentlemen," his deep voice shook with anger.

"We get that passage stricken from the records before it's printed. Once it's dispersed across Europe, they 'll know us as traitors," his brother responded.

"Yet, he said that he planned on imparting his clemency. Perhaps he is just trying to scare us." Lyon, one of the most affable of the group, tried to calm the others down.

"Not in his present mood. He's back to being as unpredictable as ever. We thought we had him in our palms and now, he's taking control over the proceedings." Unbidden, he looked over at me. Not liking what he saw, he squeezed my hand in reassurance. Unfortunately, a gesture that gave me no reassurance, nor did it calm me; instead, my anxiety continued to increase by the second

Bourbon shook his head, looking as if he were on the verge of losing his nerve. "We could speak to the Queen Mother. If anyone can temper the king's feelings, it's her."

They stood silent, silently debating their next move when another knock sounded. I jumped at the sound, hysteria causing me to think the king's Forty-Five guards were at the door, determined to arrest them for treason. Instead, it was two of Montpensier's most outspoken priests.

"The king has branded the populace of Paris as traitors! Surely you don't think his words extend only to the 'Princes of France,'" he snorted in anger.

"I can't allow the people of Paris to suffer at the hands of the king. I'll go to the Queen Mother myself in the morning to beg her to help us." Henri ran a hand through his hair, his exhaustion written on his face.

"Henri, if you had listened to me and refrained from doing things halfway in May, we would have no king to deal with." the Cardinal de Guise shook a finger in my husband's face. Horrified, I realized just how close we had come to an assassination the night he left our hotel with the Queen Mother to meet the king at the Louvre. I shuddered; my husband was no murderer. Like Montpensier, he would rather shove the king into a monastery and allow him to live out the rest of his life in disgrace. He had heeded calmer counsel and spared the king's life. Would Henri Valois do the same in his place? I prayed we never had to find out.

৩৶৩

AFTER THAT DAY, AN OMINOUS GLOOM DESCENDED UPON THE Chateau de Blois. Two days after our impromptu meeting in Bourbon's apartments, the king met with the members of the Sixteen present at Blois and promised that he would do nothing to avenge the Parisians' behavior in May. Still, something was missing. I noted that the king never made a promise to forego any punishment for the Princes of Lorraine who took part in that day. That evening, the king conferred command of the army in Poitou to my brother-in-law, the Duc de Nevers. The king made a special provision they would never force Louis to hand over his command to my husband. In the event of an uprising, the king would always have a division of the army was not under Guise control.

The Queen Mother had refused to speak with her son about censoring the lines marking my husband a traitor, so I decided that I would have to take matters into my own hands. Days had passed, and Henri grew more agitated at the thought of the rest of Europe branding him a traitor. On All Saint's Day, I rushed into her chambers and begged an audience. Sighing, she waved her attendants away.

"What may I do for you, Madame de Guise?" her voice was soft, lacking any of her typical vitriol.

"I want to ask your Majesty's help."

"How can I possibly help you? The Guise have their Assembly, your husband is in control of the Army and the Court." she sounded bored, as if she resented the burden of going through the motions of another intrigue.

"Yet, the king branded him a traitor. What he did was in defense of your son's throne. This is not the work of a traitor."

She scoffed, "Paris is in Guise hands—how is that not the work of a traitor?"

I shook my head, "Henri offered to broker a truce between the populace and the Swiss invaders." I deftly left out the French troops that the king sent pouring into the streets. "He offered several times to help the king recapture Paris. That shows his loyalty."

"People purchase loyalty cheaply these days. I have information that your husband is more loyal to Phillip of Spain than France. With the Armada destroyed, that loyalty may be up for sale again."

"Madame, it does France no good to splinter and fight. We are both threatened by Heresy. The king swore to protect his people and the church, should we not be united under those banners now?"

She waved her hand, "Perhaps. What would your husband do if of my son died?"

"We would support the only legitimate heir, my uncle, the Cardinal de Bourbon."

"Henri of Navarre has the stronger claim," she pointed a long, bony finger at me. Frailty be damned, she could still command strength when she wanted to.

"He has taken up Protestantism and refuses to acknowledge the True Church. The Edict of Union forces the king to make war on Navarre. You and I both know that makes him unworthy of the throne. His Holiness has already excommunicated him. Without the support of Rome, France could be easy pickings for invaders."

"Perhaps you are right," she stood, and I sank to my knees in obeisance. "I doubt that your cousin, Navarre will earnestly embrace the True Church as you did once. God knows that I have tried." She half-sat, half-stumbled back onto her seat. "I will speak with the king. Publicly airing factions will not help in the long run." With that, she dismissed me.

As I walked along the hallway, I saw Charlotte de Sauve coming towards me. Flushed with my victory with the Queen Mother, I had no desire to ruin my mood by engaging with my husband's whore. Henri had not spent every night at Blois with me and I was not naïve enough to think it was due to fatigue. I still held rank over a lowly Marquess and I resolved to ignore her as we passed.

"Madame la Duchesse." She, however, refused to let me go unnoticed.

"Madame de Sauve," I nodded stiffly. She bristled at the slight. "Madame de Noirmoutier. I have been so for almost two years."

"Ah, I forgot your husband, as I'm sure you have forgotten yourself."

"I see that you are with child, Madame de Guise. It is your husband's is it not? Ah, but you'll be leaving soon to give birth no doubt. Blois is bursting with people now that the Estates-General is in town." Her dig hit me, they forced us to vacate our rooms to make room for Christine of Lorraine's Medici fiancée and his family. The slight stung, but even more so when I considered it would place me far away from my husband and drive him into Charlotte's languid arms.

"I'll be leaving soon to give birth to my child, yes. I've been so blessed with children during our marriage." It was common knowledge that Charlotte had only given birth to a single healthy child. Gossip abounded that she had aborted Navarre's bastard during their liaison years before. "I would assume that you would take the time to visit your child instead of skulking around hallways looking for a lover."

She giggled, the high peel reverberating on the stone walls. "Madame, I have no need to 'look' for anything. I'm quite pleased with what I have." Anger and a wave of nausea hit me simultaneously. I would not humiliate myself by vomiting in front of a common whore. Sticking my chin out, I rushed past her and out to the courtyard. Once there, I was sick for ten minutes.

I spent the next four days packing, churlish at the thought I would leave Henri at the mercy of the king and Charlotte de Sauve. I had failed to learn who she was working for, but my instincts told me she was the king's creature, as much as she had been his Mother's. Before I left, however, the king called Henri into his presence and as the fog rolled in on an early November morning; he struck the offending words from his speech and gave him his reprieve.

⁕

"THIS RAIN IS MISERABLE. I THINK I HEARD SLEET," MONTPENSIER whined at my side. I was not thrilled to have her with me, either. Whereas I was going to Paris to settle in before I had my child, she was leaving for very different reasons. During her brief stay at Blois, she had stirred up the king's anger with her words. Henri begged me to bundle his sister into a carriage and spirit her away from the king before she wound up in a cell. "The weather is miserable, and I'm so far gone with the child I can hardly think straight. Now you want to saddle me with your sister?" I whined at him, exercising a pregnant woman's prerogative. Neither of us would spend Christmas at Blois, it seemed.

"Please," he took my hands in his and looked deeply into my eyes. Filled with the conflicting emotions of pregnancy, I could not say no to him. "I can't stand something happening to her. My mother would never forgive me if it did."

"I shall never forgive you for forcing me to ride the road from Blois to Paris with her." He kissed the top of my head and helped me into my carriage. I sighed and leaned my head back onto the head cushion as the carriage took off. I was so annoyed with him I did not bother to look back at him.

"At least we're away from that gauche, Charlotte de Sauve. She's been at every dinner since October."

"You mean the ones where your sharp tongue got you into so much trouble?" I added archly. I truly was trapped. She would crouch on my frayed nerves throughout the trip.

"I think 'Father Henri' is a good name for Henri Valois," she replied tartly. "He should take it as a compliment, considering how many pilgrimages he goes on.

"Anyway, Charlotte's looking for new prey, have you heard? She's tried sinking her claws into Mayenne. The absurdity of it all!" She burst into laughter. "She's not even the woman Charles finds attractive, but does that stop Charlotte? No!"

I had no desire to hear the latest gossip about my husband's mistress, but she pressed on. "Charles and Henri got into a huge argument over her, Charles telling him he was making a fool of himself. Henri ordered him to the yard so they could fight it out. When they got there, Charles just waved his hand and told him he was wasting his time." She gave a small shrug, "My brothers."

The season of Advent was one of the loneliest times of my life. Without the court, my husband, my remaining sister, or even my mother-in-law for company, I spent the month of December in a dark mood. My one bright spot was the time spent with Louise, who would soon be a year old, and her sister Jeanne, would all too soon grow out of being a precocious toddler. The extra time alone gave me time to reflect and quietly prepare for the new baby.

Montpensier moved into the Hotel de Guise to spend the holiday with me and we spent the day of December 23rd playing with baby Louise. "She's so serious, sometimes I can hardly believe that she's a Guise." She removed her necklace and gave the beads to Louise to suck upon. I wanted to protest, worried she would ruin the shape of her mouth by constantly sucking, but I decided that just for Christmas, we could indulge my tiny daughter.

❧

ON THE MORNING OF CHRISTMAS EVE, I WOKE EARLY TO START celebrations with my daughter. Minutes after I finished my breakfast, a sharp knock sounded at the great door of the Hotel. I knew immediately that the message must be from Blois. Sighing, I admitted that even on the day of our Lord's birth, it could not spare me the intrigues of the court.

One of Henri's teenage pages huffed into the door, his breath smoking up the hallway. "Forgive me, Madame. I rode as hard as my horse would allow." He winced as a stitch in his side caught, forcing him to take a shallow breath.

"Come by the fire and warm up. It's Christmas. I'm sure your

Mother would not forgive me if I allowed you to freeze to death." I raised my hand and tried to usher him into the antechamber, but he shook his head rapidly. He glanced around nervously, as if he would rather be anywhere else but in my presence. "Someone told me the Duchesse de Montpensier was living with you, is she here?"

My blood ran cold at his question. Why would a young man fear being alone with an emotional pregnant woman, unless he was there to impart bad news? "She is in her rooms; I will send for her." We passed the next ten minutes before Montpensier's arrival in stone silence, neither of us wanting to break the agonizing quiet. When we heard the swish of Montpensier's velvet skirts, he rose to his feet with a clatter. "Forgive me for being the one to tell you and this on the day before the celebrations of our Lord's birth." He crossed himself vigorously. I rolled my eyes and braced myself for whatever the vacillating king had laid out for Henri this time. "It's the Duc de Guise, he has..." He shook with the effort. "He is dead, Madame." Tears formed in his eyes and despite my shock, I knew that he was serious.

I blinked and clutched at the bottom of my stomach, a spasm echoing my surprise. "How? Was there an accident?"

He shook his head once again, "You should sit for this news." With him on one side and Montpensier on the other, he settled me gently into a chair. From somewhere, my lady's maid, Suzanne appeared, and she did her best to hold me until Montpensier could take over the job of consoling me.

Holding a hat that rapidly melted with snow, he told me of the horrors that had occurred the past two days. "They assassinated him, Madame, under the king's orders. We had heard murmurings that the king planned to do him harm, but no one thought His Majesty would spoil the festivities of the Duc of Tuscany's wedding. He would never dare to face the wrath of the Queen Mother." He gave me a wan smile and paused for several minutes before continuing.

Given her bouts of emotion, I expected Montpensier to gasp or fly into a rage. I do not know what passed over her face because I could not bear to look at her, but I heard only silence from her. I could not stand to sit idly by, passively accepting that my husband was gone.

Hefting all of my weight, I rose to my feet. "I want to know the details! What has that cur, Henri Valois done to him?"

The boy gulped, "He invited the Duc for an early morning meeting after breakfast. After eating his meal in the king's antechamber, they ushered the Duc into the king's most private chamber. Likely, my lord assumed it was an assurance he was being admitted into the king's most intimate confidence."

How like Henri to think he had finally achieved his goals and follow blindly into a trap. "He had no warning? No idea that his life was at risk? How could you surround him with such paltry intelligence?" The boy was blameless in this plot against my husband, but I had no care for that fact. I would lash out at Christ himself if I had been able.

"No less than five people warned him of the danger, Madame. The Duc de Mayenne warned him before he rode to Paris a week ago." I snorted, had Henri not been too busy arguing with Charles over his whore, he could have picked up on the danger surrounding him. "God damned Charlotte de Sauve! She had him ensnared in Henri Valois trap from the beginning!"

"She was one of those who warned him. If she was working for the king, she betrayed her master in the last minutes. She tried to warn the Duc of the danger he was walking into." I turned to look at Montpensier; if Charlotte was not working as a spy for the king, then who was the strumpet working for? Now was not the time to worry about her sympathies, however. I had a husband to bury.

"When will the body reach Paris? We will have to have a funeral. The people will want to mourn him." Tears pricked at my eyes and I suddenly remembered the last time I sat behind my husband's coffin. I was so young then, but then, I was not great with child. My heart ached at the thought; beneath my heart, Henri's last child lay sleeping. He or she would never be chucked under the chin by their charismatic father.

"I am so sorry, Madame. The king ordered the bodies disposed of. They burned them. They scattered the ashes into the Loire."

Montpensier snapped her head up. "What bodies? What has happened?"

"It's not just the Duc de Guise, my Lady. They also assassinated the Cardinal de Guise. You have lost two of your brothers." Her face became for a few minutes vividly suffused, although she sat motionlessly. After an interval, her cries of despair, horror, and rage resounded through the entire vast hotel. She tore her hair and in words of appalling purport, cursed the tyrant.

❧

I SHOULD NOT HAVE STOOD UP. IF I WERE IN A BETTER STATE OF mind, I would have long since taken a seat. As it was, I was still standing. Those were the last thoughts I had before the entire world went black.

❧

WHEN I WOKE, IT WAS AFTERNOON. THE THIN COLD DECEMBER SUN barely shone through the windows of my bedchamber. Montpensier came to check my forehead, placing her hand against my skin as if checking for fever. "Don't sit up," she barked at me. Defying her, I raised my head to see three of my women sitting by the bed. They had left their own families to come to my bedside.

From outside, I could hear shouting and the noise of a foaming crowd. "What's going on? Is there a riot?" One of my ladies shook her head, "No, the people wish to see if you and Madame de Montpensier are all right. They know you are here alone and they come to give their condolences."

Their concern touched me. The crowds of Paris had always been our supporters, an affinity that the Valois had never cultivated. The people warmed towards authenticity, not a feeling of entitlement. Henri Valois had thought it entitled him to end my husband's life, and the crowd rushed to see that his widow was all right. "I should go to them."

One woman shook her head, "No, the physician says you're too weak." I looked over at Montpensier, who looked just as drained as I felt. Since leaving Blois, she had experienced swelling in her extremities and now, she looked as if the condition would overwhelm her.

"Help me up, I will go to the balcony." One of them looked as if she would defy me, but I was in no mood for debate. "Up! Or I will do it myself. Would you have the people of Paris see I am bereft of my husband *and* my women!" Their shoulders slumped, and they struggled to help me to a seated position.

I could hear the angry shouts well before I opened the doors to the balcony of the hotel. Women called Henri and the Cardinal de Guise martyrs, men devoted to the survival of the church. Others shouted that the king was the antichrist. I wondered if they could hear me when I took the balcony. I needn't have worried because when the crowd saw me; they took on a hush like that during Mass. I cleared my throat, determined to gain control over my emotions.

"My heart is broken. I have lost my husband and the father of this helpless babe, who lies within me. Like you, I planned to celebrate the birth of our Lord in peace and like a good Frenchwoman. That right was taken from me just as they have taken the rights of every Parisian for the past fifteen years. Before today, I did not wholeheartedly believe that it was right to oppose an anointed king. I believed that God put Henri Valois on the throne according to his will."

I looked at my hands, realizing that at that moment, I no longer believed in anything that they had taught me my entire life. The realization took the fight out of me, draining my life essence slowly. Revolution had seemed like such a radical idea, one reserved for the mentally unbalanced and the disgruntled. Now, in that moment, I fully became one of them.

"I cannot forgive a man who ruthlessly takes the life of The King of Paris. I cannot sit idly by while he drags France into constant heresy and warfare. I know that none of you can sit idly by either." At that moment, a plan formed in my mind, but I could not give words to it. Not yet, not in front of the crowd. Unable to express the feelings inside of me, I collapsed and out of the corner of my eyes, I saw the women reaching to steady me. I barely heard the roar of the crowd as they blessed me. I meekly let them lead me from the balcony and back to my bedchamber.

As I made my way back, I heard Montpensier haltingly drag herself to the balcony. I heard snippets of her speech to the crowd, one that inflamed them further. She repeated the words she used earlier that afternoon, cursing Henri Valois. Her anguish had a reviving effect on me and for a moment, I thought to go through the streets surrounding the hotel and stir up the populace.

⚜

THE FOLLOWING DAY BEING CHRISTMAS, PARIS WOULD USUALLY BE under a dreamy spell of reflection. Christmas Day of 1588, however, was not such a day. None of us would leave the hotel to attend Christmas Mass, a break with a lifelong tradition. Instead, my personal confessor came to celebrate Mass in the Chapel of the Hotel where we said prayers for the dead through our sobs.

After our luncheon, Montpensier retired to her rooms to write her remaining brothers, chiefly Mayenne, who would inherit the role of head of the Guise family. My son was still not fifteen and not yet in his majority. He remained at Blois, under close guard, until he could escape the king's eye and find his freedom. Although I cared not one whit what happened to military power in France, the king gave my brother-in-law, Louis command of the army to keep it from falling under Mayenne's command.

The day after Christmas, Paris sprang into action to defend itself against the king and his army. I had avoided speaking with the Sixteen earlier, but they insisted on greeting me at the hotel that afternoon. I could no longer put off speaking with them, so as I sat in my black-draped drawing room, I received the men who governed Paris and for years had been close allies of my husband.

"Madame, we cannot imagine the anguish you are going through today." At his words, I inclined my head. He looked familiar, one of the indistinguishable men I had met during a salon in the rooms of this same building. Today, we reunited for a more sorrowful occasion. "No doubt His Holiness will Condémn the king for his actions at Blois. It is a shame for every Frenchman that the Princes of Lorraine are no longer with us."

"I thank God that there are still some princes left to us. My son is safe, and the Duc de Mayenne is still at liberty." From the corner or the room, I saw one of them shift his feet awkwardly. Ignoring him, I pressed on. None of them could know of the plan I was planning. There had been too many spies in their ranks before and I would risk none of them running back to the king for payment and telling him of my plan for revenge.

"My Lady, have you not heard the latest?"

I shook my head, weary of the influx of bad news from Blois. Each day, the news grew worse, and I had stopped bracing myself for even worse tidings.

"Just this morning, the king apprehended the Guise faction living in Blois. They have placed the Dowager—excuse me, your mother-in-law under guard." His slip of the tongue reminded me I was now the dowager Duchesse de Guise, not Anna.

"But, Anna d'Este is a close friend of the Queen Mother, surely the king would not dare hurt her?" At those words, I realized how ridiculous the idea sounded. Any man who ordered the slaughter of Henri de Guise would not hesitate to put his own cousin under guard, no matter how close she was to the Queen Mother. I raised my eyebrows to show my disgust at the news.

"There is more," he faltered, and another man took up the burden of telling me the rest of the news from Blois. "The king also put your son the Prince of Joinville under guard. For now, he is safe, and we don't think he is an imminent danger."

I sank back in my chair in despair. I had hoped that Charles would make it to Normandy to fortify himself at Eu. With the Jesuits residing on the estate, he could plan his next move in safety. Now, he was at the king's mercy.

"I'm sorry, I meant the *Duc de Guise* is under guard." Until the man spoke, I had not still not realized that my eldest son was now the new Duc de Guise, a boy with no real experience in leadership, but already the weight of his family's inheritance on his slim shoulders. I was the Dowager Duchesse de Guise, a title I had associated with Anna for so long it felt as if she had always held it. Now it was up to me to take up the Guise legacy and honor my husband.

"My Lady, you seem disturbed. We have come here to assure you you will always have the support of the people of Paris. We have resolved that we will take responsibility for your and the Duc's children."

It sounded like an empty promise coming from these men, these would-be politicians. I had felt this sentiment, a sincere expression of sympathy, from the people the other day on the balcony. In that moment, coming from these men, it sounded hollow and easily discarded at will. Unwilling to let them know of my true feelings, I inclined my head. "That is very generous of you."

"That is not all. If, God willing, your child is a boy, the city pledges to stand beside him at the baptismal font and serve as a godparent."

I lifted my eyebrows, "The entire city. Your charity is remarkable." Weeks ago, I had hoped to repair my rift with Henriette by asking her to become my child's godmother. Her silence made that wish seem unlikely to come true.

"We are striving to free those dear to you. The Cardinals of Bourbon and Lyon are also under guard. The king has sequestered himself behind his chamber walls with the queen and the Duchess of Tuscany. The Queen Mother," he hesitated and glanced around at his compatriots, "is in declining health. No one expects her to live out the year."

I crossed myself at hearing the words. My last audience with Catherine de Medici came to me, my desperate negotiations to save Henri's reputation. She resigned herself to the inevitable that day, knowing that her life was rapidly ending. Even enveloped in my grief, I mourned the demise of the woman who had led the court for thirty years. With her death, the ing would lose his one remaining ally.

Realizing that, I knew that with her death the king was even more isolated than before; if that were possible. After alienating himself from the bulk of his subjects, he had few real friends left to mourn his own demise. Still, every time I had thought the king defeated, he came back defiant. I would never underestimate his power again.

❧ 8 ❧

The king crowed in his chambers he was finally master of France, but as the vast Guise relations planned a revolt and his mother's life drained from her, he also lost his own vitality. The men remaining at Blois remarked that the king seemed lesser each day than the one before. Yet the king worked to keep his enemies under close watch. They transferred my eldest son and mother- to the stronger prison at the Chateau d'Amboise. Anna could not get any letters to us, but her women reported that she spent the days in prayer for her dead sons and for the draining life of Catherine de Medici.

The young Duc de Nemours, alone, escaped the transfer from Blois to Amboise and he reached Paris on the 13th of January. The king had toyed with releasing Anna, but once he realized her son was at liberty, he kept her under key, to keep her from conspiring with Mayenne and Montpensier. By the sixteenth of January, the king dismissed the Estates-General and the experiment of democracy was over. We lay in wait for the king's next move that would likely involve striking at Paris.

A day later, I awoke to find that I was bleeding. Terrified that I would lose my child, I took to my bed and prayed for a safe delivery. I could not stand the heartache of losing Henri's child so soon after losing him. My body could never withstand the stress of a stillbirth.

Unable to do anything more, I resolved to stay out in my rooms and remain patient until the child came. When he was safely in his crib, I would resume plotting.

On Monday, January 30th, they performed a grand requiem in Notre Dame for the Duc de Guise and his brother. They hung the churches of the capital with black; and for the entire day, Paris remained prostrate, fasting, and weeping the demise of her hero. There were no bodies for us to bury, only ashes floating in the Loire. Still fearful of losing my child, I could not attend and Montpensier and the Duc d' Aumale attended in my place. It was just as well I was not there; I would have shamed myself by dissolving into tears.

At Amboise, the king alienated himself even from the captain of the Forty-Five and du Gaust, the jailer of the Guise dynasty. At the beginning of February, he finally gave my mother-in-law her freedom. His timing could not have been more fortuitous because my child would enter the world at any moment.

On February 7th, my labor finally began. After bringing thirteen previous children from my womb, the experience of childbirth no longer caused me anxiety. I still worried that the horror of December would be an ill omen for the child. Twelve hours after I felt the first stirring, the midwife pronounced that I had a son. He was small and gave out a small cry, but otherwise, he was healthy. The people would have you believe that he came into the word with his hands clasped in supplication and with eyes raised to heaven. That is a silly myth meant to stir up the people, I can assure you. He came into the world wiggling, just as any other babe before him.

The next day, the people of Paris fulfilled their promise to act as godparents for my new son. Henriette, unwilling to communicate with me, the Duchesse d'Amuale stood as his godmother. At the altar of St. Jean de Grève, the place of worship for the Guise family, I named him Alexandre Paris. The christening completed, several men rose to expound on the behavior of the tyrant who ended this child's beloved father's life. To show their regard for me, many stopped to give presents to my son. One, in particular, held my interest. "Ambassador Mendoza." He took my hand once I could free it from under Alexandre's wriggling body. Kissing it as if I were Queen Louise herself, he took his own hand and pressed it on top of mine.

"My great Lady, words cannot express how I feel at your loss." Although I had little time to waste on pleasantries, for Alexandre's sake, I accepted his condolences. I also pressed my case. I had plans for Mendoza and the Spanish.

"I would like to meet with you at the Hotel de Guise." Despite his years of subterfuge at the English and French courts, he could not hide his surprise at my request.

"It would honor me." He made a show of bowing to the Dowager Duchesse de Guise and her fatherless child. France and Spain united, that was what I had in mind.

⁂

AT THE END OF THE WEEK, MY CHAMBERLAIN USHERED MENDOZA into the study. "I won't delay you; instead, I will come right to my point. I want to arrange a marriage between Phillip's daughter, Catalina and my son, the Duc de Guise." It was perfect timing, as Charles' previously betrothed had died of the plague last summer. Burdened with the issues of statecraft, Henri and I had delayed arraigning another match for our heir. The solution came soon after I heard of the slaughter of my husband.

"I will send word to His Majesty immediately. He is entertaining several matches for his daughter."

I snorted, "I am sure he is. With Bourbon in captivity, he is hardly a suitable candidate to succeed as King of France. Catalina is the king's niece, carrying both Valois and Hapsburg blood. Along with my son's heritage as a direct descendant of the Capets, there are few who could match his pedigree."

"His Majesty has asked that the Infanta Catalina be put forth as the League claimant to the throne." There had been plans in motion to remove the Salic law that forbade women inheriting, along with specific language barring Margot from inheriting after her brother's death. Taking advantage of this, Phillip had put forth his unmarried daughter as a candidate take the throne.

"The French people may not accept a Spanish princess as their queen, but if she married a French prince, I cannot see any reason they would reject her. Convey to Phillip that this marriage would be to both our advantage."

He took a sip of the wine in front of him, "Madame—I believe it just might."

❦

"THE NERVE OF THAT CLUMSY, DIRT-COVERED BUMPKIN!" I THREW down the paper and stomped on it to stop it from offending me further. Determined to push his case for the French throne, Navarre opened the month of March by decrying the movements of both the king and the League. As ever, the king hid in his chateau at Blois, too timid to return to Paris. Reeling from Henri's death, the remaining leaders of the League tried to rally their troops under Mayenne's command.

My brother-in-law was proving to be a less than inspiring commander. Dawdling in Paris and gorging on food, he refused to expand the League's control over the south and center of the country. In this vacuum of power, marched Navarre, solidifying the south under Protestant rule throughout that spring. France was in danger of splitting into two nations, one in the south, ruled by an absolute king, and one to the north, ruled by a burgeoning constitutional government. While the king feared the damage a constitution would do to his rule, he did not act to curb the League's power in the north. This made getting messages to and from Eu easier than they had been in a decade.

Between his own whoring and soldering, Navarre had taken the time to print and distribute a proclamation decrying the Spanish support of the League and the push for representative government springing up across France. While his fellow Protestants might structure their religious meetings in a democratic flavor, make no mistake about his designs for ruling France. Navarre would rule as one and over all of France once given the chance.

I wanted to keep him from doing so. Once Charles and the Infanta married, France would have two strong Catholics on the throne and two who not influenced by unworthy bumpkins as Henri Valois was. Spanish stock may have plummeted since the destruction of the Armada the previous Summer, but Spain was still a powerful ally. A powerful ally I wanted to win to our side.

There was virtually nothing left of the Parlement of Paris, which officially ruled the city. Everyone knew that the Sixteen ruled in theory and practice. Still, I went to the Parlement in late March to present an official petition to begin proceedings against all the men responsible for the death of my husband and his younger brother. I knew that the trail would immediately lead them to investigate the king, and I relished the image of them squirming when presenting a warrant against the king. To my surprise, the Parlement was more than willing to grant a petition to such an "illustrious widow" and they sat about appointing commissioners to start proceedings against Henry Valois and his co-conspirators. I hoped that I would receive justice.

The Parlement went even further than granting my petition; in January, we learned that the Pope had granted absolution for the murders of the Guise brothers. The idea was abhorrent and to any right-thinking Catholic in France. With his actions, the Pope had made clear his decision to move towards the king and betray the League he himself had supported for years.

⚜

In April, Mendoza finally received an answer from Phillip regarding my offer of marriage between Charles and the Infanta Catalina. As I read Mendoza's response, anger boiled up inside me. "His Most Catholic Majesty is not convinced that an alliance with the house of Lorraine is the best match for his eldest daughter. He wishes to unite her with a Hapsburg prince, under the tradition of the House of Hapsburg. In addition, as the League is unwilling to commit to preserving the Catholic faith, he wonders if the house of Lorraine is as strong as it once was."

I gritted my teeth—of course, the house of Lorraine was not as strong as it once was. In November, it had a strong leader, and a committed commander who could lead it to glory. Now, reduced to a corpulent third son who was showing himself to be a complete coward. My son might not be old enough to lead the Guise family, but within three years he would be. He would show himself to be just as effective as his late father had been. He would be another military giant, a man worthy to be called the son of Guise.

Grabbing a piece of paper, I jabbed at it until I had composed a response to Mendoza.

"Might I remind Phillip that Spanish power has diminished since last August? Marriage to another Hapsburg will mean that a hostile France remains between Spain and Austria. Such an alliance would yield no advantage to Phillip, only maintain the status quo. France hungers after a strong leader and one who has not dedicated himself to the Heretic cause."

Wounding Phillip's pride and reminding him of the spreading cancer of Protestantism might well be enough to scare the Spanish king into a commitment. I hastily sealed the letter and sent it on to Mendoza's house.

I immediately composed a missive to Eu, demanding that the priest who caused the rift between Henriette and I come to my house in Paris as soon as possible. It was time to put my plan into action. Navarre felt the crown of France sitting upon his dirty head.

In April, Navarre and the king formalized an alliance, putting down their arms and signing a treaty outside of Tours. Without the two men opposing one another, there was only one enemy left for them both to face: the Catholics of the League. Once the two armies combined, there was nothing to stop them from marching upon Paris. Henri Valois would take his revenge upon the city, and now he would do so with the help of hundreds of Protestant troops under Navarre's command.

There was nothing left to stop those troops but Mayenne. Finally, he had to admit that his laziness had led to this watershed moment. Had he acted months earlier, as so many had begged him to do so, the job might have been easier. Gathering up as many men as he could, he began a slow campaign to clear the road between Paris and the city of Tours. Although I was angry at Mayenne for not acting sooner, I felt safe enough in Paris with the wall of men between us and the king's combined army. Mayenne would keep the fighting well away from us. Alexandre was still a symbol of pride for the League and I felt justified in keeping him and his sisters, Louise and Jeanne with me in the city. Besides, only a coward would run away to either Joinville or Eu.

Even more so, I had a plan for breaking the king and his newfound alliance with Navarre. To carry out that plan, Father Jean came from Eu to repay his longstanding debt to me. "Father, I trust your 'sisters' are happily settled in France?" As with the Sixteen, I sat in state under a drapery of black, emphasizing my status as Duchesse de Guise. Until Catalina married my son, I would continue to use that title to my advantage. Given how much this man had cost me, I would make sure he quaked before me.

Recognizing his status, he looked down at his feet in shame. "I am sorry, Madame. I should not have deceived you."

"No, you should not have. Since you already have, you will now make up for your sins against me."

He gulped, fear written across his face. "How so, My Lady?"

"I understand that the Jesuits are skilled in combat and taking care of problems. I want you to take care of a particular problem I have had recently." I needed say no more, he knew what task I had set for him.

"This is for the survival of the Holy Church. I will see to it someone forgives you for your deed." If Rome could absolve the king, then His Holiness could do the same for the man who avenged Henri Valois' crime.

❧

ALTHOUGH THE GUISE CAUSE REVELED IN THE ABSENCE OF THE KING, eventually cracks appeared within the family. The unity that Henri cultivated for so long was splintering after his death. I blame that fully on Mayenne's lack of leadership skills. Unlike his older brothers, he was indecisive, lazy, and more invested in furthering his own means than that of the family. His behavior caused many of them to wonder if he was worth following at all.

As it was, he could barely install a stable government within Paris itself. The men he installed to govern the city immediately passed legislation cutting taxes. While the poor reveled in the break-in taxa-tion, eventually the middle-class lost money. Within months, the city's economy started a slow ruin.

The women of the family wedged divisions between ourselves. Previously, Anna d'Este had been available to curb her daughter's fits of emotion, but after the death of her eldest sons, she retired to her country estate to hover over her eldest son by the Duc de Nemours. Determined to avoid watching another son fall to an assassination by making up for the years of lost motherhood, she smothered her son at the expense of tending to her Guise children. Her absence led to building resentment.

No one resented her absence more than her only daughter. Mont-pensier continued to rail against the king, and amid her complaints against the king, she spoke against her missing mother. Somehow, she found the time to badger her brother into taking up arms against the king and marching towards Blois. Had it not been for her, I doubt that he would ever deign to leave Paris.

Once he did, she changed her tone to praising him in the highest notes. "With him goes the strongest chance for a united France," she faced me one warm day in the middle of April.

I shrugged, "*If* he goes all the way to Blois. He seems half-hearted at best."

"He's a worthy successor to the crown. He should take it the moment he defeats Brother Henri." I bit my lower lip; if she honestly thought the king could peacefully enter a monastery after his crimes against the Guise, she was mistaken.

Anger flared at me. Was she truly going mad? "Mayenne? The third son? When he has several nephews who have a better claim to the throne? If it goes to a Guise, it should rightly go to my son, Charles." I ignored the superior claim of the son of the Duc de Lorraine, who was also a grandchild of Henry II and Catherine de Medici. Given the city's love for Henri, his son would be the sentimental favorite.

"He seems very un-kinglike. He may prove to be an effective soldier, but he, in general, is unremarkable." She waved her hand as if debating the merits of a pastry.

"Your own nephew, the Duc de Guise, you dare call him 'unremarkable'? How dare you? You, a woman with no children, have the nerve to call my son 'unremarkable'?" I shouted at her, venting my full wrath. Anyone else would quake at my yelling, but Montpensier was nonplussed.

"I'm only stating a fact. The people will see it, too. Eventually." She gave a small shrug. So, this was the extent of Montpensier's loyalty—once her beloved brother was out of the picture, she owed it to no one.

"I think it's time you retired for the faubourgs." I snapped at her, unwilling to stand her presence one second longer.

By the end of the week, people overheard Montpensier making the case for Mayenne to take the French throne. As she had with me, she smoothly disregarded my son's stronger claim as the eldest son of the eldest son. With the throne up for grabs, we could disregard any pedigree.

To my amusement, she also threatened the king's safety, in words so inflammatory, that the king sent a gentleman of his bedchamber to tell her that her words were treasonous. If she were wise, the message read, to retire from Paris and thus save herself from death by fire.

Montpensier stayed put in Paris, to mine and the king's disappointment. At a party held in the Paris City Hall, she shouted that she would do anything to prevent the king from returning to Paris. I did not temper her speech; she was proving to be more helpful than she knew.

$\maltese$ *9* $\maltese$

t the end of April, a letter finally arrived from Henriette. Louis rejected at an alliance with the Protestant troops and had retired to Nevers in protest. Finally, Louis and I were in agreement about something and I took it as a step towards reconciliation. I hoped that my sister would never learn about my plans for the king, but if we could repair our relationship, I would be grateful.

Louis' departure from Blois meant that the king turned to his habitual advisor, the Duc d'Épernon. Hearing the news, I seethed. Henri had worked for years to remove the sycophant from the king's council and now that Louis had left in disgust, Épernon was back.

"I've been too quick to judge you and now I cannot think of you in Paris without Henri. As much as we often disagreed regarding the king, I regarded him as a friend. His loss is immeasurable." I teared up as I read Henriette's letter. I finally had my sister back. Letters also arrived from Blois, carrying the king's seal. The Guise women, including Montpensier and I, would immediately leave Paris and lodge at Blois. I could see through the king's words. Unlike in the past, this would not be an invitation to serve at court. We were to go under guard, just as Anna had been during the chilly months of winter. She had barely escaped and there was little chance I would.

I laughed as I read the letter from the king. This ruse reminded me too much of his meeting with Henri at Blois in December. I would not need five people to warn me that to leave for Blois was suicide. I would rather die than allow the king to put me under custody. Nothing would compel me to leave Paris and the support of the people. I was safe in Paris and so were my children. If Mayenne failed, Paris would defend itself against an army headed by Navarre and the king.

Another letter arrived the next day, written in Queen Louise's own hand. In it, she begged me to ride to Blois so that the king and his guard could ensure my safety. They had received word at Blois that Paris was collapsing under a ruined economy. The royal troops would march into the city soon to restore order and chaos would result. She could not guarantee my safety in Paris, but under guard at Blois, I would protect my youngest children and myself. I shook my head at her words. Previously, Henri Valois had not used the queen to entrap her own family. She had been off limits in attacking the king. Now, he stooped to using her as a weapon to capture the remaining members of the Guise family. The letter Louise sent to Anna was even more manipulative; she addressed her as the mother of two dead sons and inferred that her remaining children from her Guise and Nemours marriages were now in peril.

Thank God, Henriette and I had reconciled, because even in Nevers, she was not immune to plotting. At the end of April, a fanatical preacher ascended the pulpit in the cathedral of Nevers and preached a sermon filled with the foulest abuse against the king. The words were familiar, sounding like the priests Montpensier patronized in Paris. Louis sat the sermon out, then sent for the monk and forced him to return to the pulpit and contradict each of his previous assertions. Regardless of his issues with the King, Louis would allow no one to incite a riot under his nose.

To my relief, after Louis stormed into the palace in fury, Henriette sent a letter urging me to remain in Paris. My sister knew full well that my life was in danger if I were to take the king's offer and head towards Blois. I thank God that she knew that I was blameless this time in the plotting.

ON THE FIRST WEEK OF MAY, MAYENNE FINALLY MARCHED UPON the outskirts of Tours. The city was the traditional Viscountcy of Charlotte de Sauve's family, ruled over by Charlotte and her latest husband. The former whore of both Navarre and my husband, now stood to lose her lands, an ironic touch I found amusing. She had been so arrogant for years, parading her charms and her ability to lure men to her bed, and now, she was powerless to stop the army outside her city. If Charlotte was among the dead, I would not mourn her loss one bit.

As I sat in Paris, awaiting the result of the campaign against Tours, a knock sounded at the door of my chamber. "Madame, there is a priest waiting to see you." Wrinkling my brow, I waved the man inside. It was Father Jean. I held my breath, willing him to give me good news.

"Madame, I have been thinking about the task you set for me." I curled my fingers, biting my palms with my fingernails. He would back out of the task.

"While the Jesuits do not shirk from their duty to defend the Holy Church, I think there is a flaw in your plan."

"A flaw? How so, Father?"

"The king well knows that the Jesuits are allies of his enemies in the League. To pass undetected, I would need to shed the clothes of a Jesuit."

"I see." His logic was sound. Sending a Jesuit into the king's camp might arouse suspicion. I did not want to fail in my plan. Relieved that he was not backing out of the task I set before him, I will listen to his argument.

"The king has been generous towards the Franciscan friars, staying with them for several of his pilgrimages. We know his affinity for their order." I nodded, finding no logic with his argument.

"Dressed as a Franciscan, I could avoid suspicion. The king would easily admit me into his private accommodations. After the tragedy of the Duc's death, I would expect the king's guards to surround him closer than ever. It's not out of the question to expect that there will be a plot to avenge the Duc's death."

"I want nothing to ruin my plan. Get into the king's confidence however you can. If someone catches you, then say you do what you're doing for the League."

He gave a curt nod and left. I wondered if I would see him before he left Paris. Mayenne's troops had secured the road between Tours and Paris, so he should have no problem reaching the king's encampment.

I spent the rest of the day waiting for the post and the message that Mayenne had surrounded the king's forces. Although he and Navarre had signed an informal truce, they would still separate their forces. Navarre camped far from the king, for his own safety. None of the Protestants trusted the man suspected of orchestrating a massacre of Protestants in the St. Bartholomew's Day Massacre in 1572 with the life of their remaining military leader. Condé might have died under suspicious circumstances, but the Protestants would not allow the same tragedy to strike them twice. In the event of a disaster, the alliance with the Catholic, Henri Valois would quickly dissolve.

After supper, I went to visit Alexandre at the nursery. He dozed peacefully, but I wanted to hold him, to remind myself of why I had done what I did. I was the only parent left to care for him and the rest of our children. Henri could no longer negotiate with fathers to make great matches that would keep him and his descendants safe. That was my duty as his mother. This was my attempt to keep him and his siblings safe.

❦

EARLY THE NEXT MORNING, A MESSAGE FINALLY ARRIVED FROM Tours. From the boy's crestfallen face, I knew that the news was bad. "The Duc could not capture Tours, My Lady. The Protestants sent for reinforcements and they arrived before he could penetrate the city."

"And the king's troops?"

"The king and his troops remain camped in Tours. There were heavy casualties on our side, but the king is still master of Tours."

I groaned and rubbed my eyebrows with my hands. Depending on how bad the casualties were, Mayenne could fall back and regroup.

There was every chance he could make up for this debacle later. If Henri were still alive, he would know how to avenge this disaster, just as he had in November after Coutras. Henri cut down the Protestants, scattering them all the way back to Switzerland. His brother could do the same. I smugly realized that with this defeat, the shine dulled on Mayenne in his candidacy for the Crown. A recalcitrant leader with a stinging defeat would be less palatable than an untried teenager. Charles had yet to prove himself on the battlefield, but unlike his uncle, he had no stinging defeats attached to his name.

THE DAYS FOLLOWING MAYENNE'S DEFEAT IN TOURS; HE FELL BACK and besieged smaller towns to encircle the revived Royal troops. His efforts were for nothing. Frenchmen daily arrived to join the royal standard, and expressions of sympathy and promised aid reached the king from England and eastward from Switzerland. Allies, who would not have dared touch the king, finally came to rally to his standard. Make no mistake; these new supporters did not declare their affiliation because of the king's chances of keeping his crown. No, they believed that Navarre would succeed him to the throne. With the two allied, supporting one meant supporting the other. More and more people accepted that Navarre represented the future.

Not our family. We would never accept my heretic cousin as our next king. As the Royalist army made its laborious march from Tours to the gates of Paris, we dug in and made plans to defend the city at all costs. At the end of May, Anna came to my home to see how Alexandre and his older sisters were progressing. Too innocent to understand the catastrophes that threatened them, they provided the only respite I had from my anxiety that summer.

"It's quite a contrast to see a nursery within such heavily fortified walls." She glanced out the window to see the guards watching over the courtyard. Although she tried to keep her voice light, it shook with concern.

"I can't remember the last time that this was a noble home. It feels as if it's been a fortress for years." It had, starting in 1586, when the king's remaining brother died, and we realized that Navarre was inching closer to the throne. Henri had done everything he could to keep Navarre from becoming king. He had given his life to the cause of keeping an unworthy man from ruling France. Only we remained to pick up his cause, one that was faltering since his incompetent brother lost his best chance to take the king hostage.

"To be honest, I'm worried what the constant warfare is doing to you and the children. I think you should send them to Joinville." My shoulders slumped at her suggestion. Only weeks earlier, it would have been an easy feat to send them from Paris to Lorraine on the main roads. Mayenne had held that same road wide open for the League. Now, however, the king and his Protestant forces were inching closer to Paris, making travel in and out of the city hazardous.

I shook my head, "Alexandre is a powerful symbol of hope for the people. If I send him away, it will all but be admitting defeat. That will betray everything that my Henri stood for. I will not tarnish his legacy by acting a coward."

"Then, at least send Louise from Paris." I looked at the gurgling toddler. She placed her fingers into her mouth, sucking on them. Mundane issues crowded my head, none the least was my annoyance at the thought she would become a thumb sucker if I did not take things into my own hands. Could I spare Louise and send her to Joinville and away from me?

"Do you think it's come to this?" Dread settled over me like a heavy blanket.

She nodded, her face clouded. "I think we've waited too long to counter the king. He took the time to add to his army. It's getting harder every day to find financial support for the League."

Playing upon my public role as the shattered, cloistered widow, I had neglected to keep up with what was happening with the League's finances. If the cause was not attracting donors, then they were rapidly losing faith in our ability to prevail. That was a powerful symbol of the temperature of the feeling of the country.

"I've done all that I can as the mother of the martyrs to raise funds. I've sold a few jewels from my Grandmother." My heart sank at the desperation and wistfulness in her voice. The jewels she inherited from her mother, Queen Anne of France were invaluable. If she had resorted to selling them, then even she was out of options.

"You should take Louise and Jeanne, then. Keep them safe in Joinville. If I'm captured, I must face the consequences. Both of the children would be safe in their grandmother's care." Although I knew that, I could not sever the tie I had with Alexandre. He was all that kept me from descending into radicalism. If they discovered my plot, I would face a sentence of treason.

Weeks earlier, the king had threatened me if I did not leave Paris for his custody at Blois. I had laughed in derision at being taken to Blois in disgrace. With Mayenne licking his wounds and barely able to regroup, I had lost my only chance to escape the king's revenge. If I fled to Joinville or tried to take the king's offer and go to Blois, I would lose my opportunity to avenge Henri's death. I could not risk telling Anna of my plans. I had to remain in Paris and play my last card in this game. Yet, this game was so lethal I could not justify exposing my newborn son to danger.

"Take all the children with you. I will remain in Paris. They may criticize me for sending Alexandre away, but will tell the people it is because the king has allied with a heretic and endangered even the most innocent of us."

❧

PARIS WAITED, HOLDING ITS COLLECTIVE BREATH THAT SUMMER. June brought superficial victories, the capture of small villages by Mayenne and his troops. It also brought a new wave of Catholic refugees, fleeing the destruction wrought by Navarre's Protestant army. The heat of Summer settled in, turning the city into a cauldron. Heartbroken, I packed up the children with their nurses for the flight to Joinville. "They'll be safe away from the city. It's obvious that Navarre is dead set on besieging the city," Anna tried to reassure me, as she settled the children into her carriage. At the sight of me bursting into tears, she took me in her arms and hugged me tightly.

"Have faith. France will never accept a Protestant as her king. God himself will save us and the country." Although she meant to calm me, her words sent me into a fresh fit of sobs. She gently disentangled herself from me and stepped into the carriage. I watched through tears, as they rolled across the courtyard and through the inner gates of the hotel. I had neglected to watch Henri the last time I saw him, and I refused to repeat my mistake.

A letter arrived from Nevers, another one from Henriette. Neither she nor Louis would fight alongside Navarre and his Protestants, a decision that led to many Catholics across France to flee to safety with us in Paris. I was angry to learn that these cowards would not fight with us against the king. As far as it concerned them, he was their lawful sovereign and they would keep their stated neutrality.

The one bright spot that June was the capture of two royal advisors in a small village outside of Paris. The Sixteen thought the two men were spies and once they apprehended them, announced that they would publicly execute them. With their capture, I saw an opening for Father Jean, one I could to capitalize upon. I ran to the home of Monsieur Caravans, the new President of the Sixteen to plead to pause their executions.

"Monsieur, I need to speak with those men."

"Madame de Guise, it is not my desire to deny you anything. Yet, I must know, why would you need to speak with them?"

"They told me that these men helped to plan my husband and brother-in-law's murder. I want to speak to them in person. It's the only way I can process my husband's death." Lies, but I had vowed long before, to never trust the Sixteen with any confidences.

"It's likely that anything they would tell you would be inappropriate for a noblewoman's ears."

"Still, my soul won't quiet until I can look in the eyes of my husband's murderers."

Finally, he relented, unable to say no to a grieving widow.

GETTING INTO THE CELL WHERE THE MEN WERE BEING HELD WAS easier than I had hoped. Few people in Paris would dare cross the wife of the slain Duc de Guise. When I went to see the first man, he had the decency to look at his feet in shame. "Madame de Guise, I am sorry for your loss."

"Spare me your sympathy, had you advised the king to take another path, you would not need to give me any condolences." I fixed a cold stare upon him.

"I have spoken with a confessor with the Franciscan order. He has advised me I should forgive the king. I have written to him to tell him of my forgiveness. I need you to write the king that I have forgiven him.

"His eyebrows shot up, but he did not deny my request. A few hours later, I had a letter from two of the king's remaining advisors. As soon as possible, I sent for Father Jean. Now, he had the means of getting into the king's confidence without arousing suspicion.

❧

THE LEAGUE WAS RUNNING OUT OF SUPPORT OUTSIDE OF FRANCE. The Pope refused to absolve the League from damnation if of the king's death. I worried if this would destroy my plot. Would Father Jean disappear with the money I paid him and refuse the risk of damnation for ridding me of the king? If so, I would lose my chance for revenge.

❧

AT MASS ONE SUNDAY IN JUNE, MONTPENSIER STOOD BY MY SIDE and glanced nervously at the crowd. "It's time to rid ourselves of that tyrant. Only his death will suffice."

I raised my eyebrows, shocked that she would speak so vehemently in a house of God. "Are you ready to put the king into a monastery now?"

She snorted, "Past time. We need a more permanent solution." To my horror and delight, she said the last sentence loud enough to cause the surrounding people to turn their heads towards us. She did not know of my plans against the king and she was unknowingly implicating herself before the people.

I would continue to play the moral and grieving widow. Mustering as much shock as possible, I turned to her, "I do not think it is very Christian-like to advocate killing the last Valois. Haven't we had enough bloodshed as it is? I, for one, am tired of it all." I crossed myself and pinched the underside of my elbow to make myself cry. At my side, Montpensier sighed in annoyance.

I felt no guilt in throwing Montpensier to the wolves. She had already earned my anger for doubting that my son could lead the Guise family into the future. Everyone in Paris had heard her rail against the king on multiple occasions. If the priest implicated me in the plot to kill the king, I would declare to all that I was only a grieving widow. I felt no guilt over framing her for the king's demise; she had earned it. She had no children to grieve her if the king put her to death.

THE KING AND NAVARRE CONTINUED TO ADVANCE TOWARDS PARIS, surrounding the city the last week of July. The city could not hold out more than a few months. Out there somewhere, was the man who would exact my revenge and rid me of the king. I had to be patient for him to know the right time to make his move.

On a sweltering second day of August, I was listless, endlessly pacing the hallways of Hotel de Guise. Something told me that the world had changed, but I would not celebrate just yet. I had to know that my instincts were right. At mid-morning, a messenger came galloping into the courtyard, yelling the news. "The king is dead! Henri Valois is no more!" I clapped my hands in relief, then crossed myself. I could not appear to be too excited at the prospect of the king's demise.

The assassin had made two attempts to kill the king. Turned away the first day, he returned to speak to his sovereign, claiming that he had letters from traitors to the League who would offer to swing Paris' gates wide open to him. Unable to resist the temptation of an easy victory, he led the man in. Handing him the letters written by the two advisors, he gained the king's confidence quickly. I don't know if he bothered to mention my gesture of reconciliation, but I suppose, it was best they not attach my name to the plot.

Flashing a blade in, what I hope, was a scene very much reminiscent of the murder of my husband, he stabbed the king, finding vital tissue with his first attempts. The king grabbed the blade to disarm him, but the damage was already done. Henri Valois, king of France, had only hours to live. As much as I worried about Father Jean giving me up as a co-conspirator, the Forty-Five took care of that problem for me. In seconds, he lay dead, unable to tell anyone about his motives. Unless he had told his mission to anyone else, I could walk away from this deed with no repercussions. I would later learn that his name was not even Jean, yet another lie he had told me. His real name was Jacques Clement and the fact I could not give even his real name meant that my alibi was even stronger than I had hoped.

Arrogant to the last and unable to accept the reality of his situation, the king immediately dictated a letter to Queen Louise at Chenonceau, telling her he was only injured and that he would live. As the day wore on, he called Navarre to his bedside. There, Henri Valois violated French and Church law by naming the heretic Navarre the heir to the throne. When the League's leaders heard of this abomination, they were livid.

Henri Valois bled to death, lying like the coward he was in his own bed. The man who masterminded the slaughter of the Huguenots in 1572 and was directly responsible for the death of my husband, finally lay dead himself. I could finally rest now I had eliminated the threat of the last Valois. The threat of the Bourbon was negligible; no Frenchman would accept Navarre as his king.

EPILOGUE

Virtually from the moment she heard of the King's death, Montpensier took credit for hiring the man to do the deed. I needn't bother denying my guilt; she was more than capable of framing herself with no help on my part. The printers in Paris went with her story, depicting her as the avenging angel, who killed the King in her grief over the loss of her brothers. If anything, it bolstered her celebrity status across France as she became known as the killer of the King. The more she sought the spotlight, the more I took strides to avoid it. Although there was a push for Navarre to become King, his wife languished under lock and key, so there was no court to speak of. I had ample time to tend to family affairs.

With the need to reunite with my children as my excuse, I quietly slipped out of Paris much as the King had done a year earlier. I traveled to Joinville, to see my children. Rumors said Navarre would march for Paris next, but it would take time before he could position his troops to attack us. I would be in Lorraine by then. I left Paris with only months to spare. Navarre began a long and unsuccessful siege that lasted longer than anyone would have imagined. He would not enter the city as its King until 1594.

Charles and I hoped he would marry the Spanish Infanta and

become King in Navarre's stead until 1593. As rulers of Lorraine, the reformed Parliaments of Paris deemed the Guise foreigners and thus, barred from the French succession. The ruling also meant that a Spanish princess was not an option, so the young Duc de Guise married a daughter of the Duc de Joyeuse. Checkmated, I returned to court in 1593 to find that Navarre planned to make his mistress, Gabrielle d'Estrees, Queen of France in Margot's stead. Relieved that there was finally a royal court in Paris once again, I returned to Paris to seek our fortunes once again. In a few years, even Louise Marguerite and Alexandre Paris would need to marry. Without a father to guide them, I was all that they had left.

THE END

of

FATE'S MISTRESS

Join Laura du Pre's mailing list to receive a **free book**, the latest news about upcoming releases, and special offers just for subscribers.

Read on for more books by this author, historical notes, and contact information.

November 1587

Henri cursed the luck that had brought him this far. He cursed his stupidity that had forced him to leave a victorious battlefield to convalesce. He had the Catholics on the run, scattered and without a leader, and now he was forced to flee too . Each mile of the pockmarked road north of Coutras was agony on his aching side.

"Water," he could barely groan out the word. Cold winds whipped at the makeshift wagon, cutting into his skin despite the coverings his men had placed around him. Those winds told him that winter would arrive any day now, forcing his army to take shelter until Spring. The elements would have forced his men to leave the battlefield eventually, but his absence left his cousin's Protestant forces without a strong leader. Not that Henry of Navarre was terribly worried about a missed opportunity to wage war against the Catholics. Leaving the battlefield meant that his cousin could spend more time with his mistress. "Go spend the time with your woman, cousin, and I will spend it with mine." A month after his victory, the Prince of Conde was forced into his bed, barking his displeasure at his men, but he could not ignore the order from Navarre. An order from his king and kinsman could not be ignored.

Thus he was shuttled into a surplus wagon on the unkept road north towards La Rochelle, and north to Protestant territory. North towards his wife. His wife—he struggled to recall the face of the woman who shared his name, this latest Princess de Conde. A quiet girl barely not even out of her teens, who would welcome him home after the laborious two days that it took to make it home to his chateau at Saint-Jean-d'Angély.

"My Lord, you should be lying down," Charles Videau, the surgeon who insisted upon coming with him on this trip clucked his displeasure at Henri's attempt to sit up.

"Dammit, man—I am thirsty. My side is being torn apart, at least you can allow me a bit of water!" Henri's mood, black and sullen had only gotten worse with each mile. He had long since stopped caring if it bothered anyone else.

"Ho! Halt the wagon!" Videau's booming voice called the procession to a halt. The wagon's jerking to a stop pitched Henri forward before he could brace himself. He grimaced at the pain.

"Forgive me, highness." Where the man managed to find his cheerfulness escaped Henri. But then, he did not have to deal with a hole carved into the side of his torso. "I know it's painful, but the stitches are managing to hold. In a couple of days, you'll be safe in a warm bed."

"Any news from the front? From my cousin Navarre?" At the guilty faces around him, Henri's mood darkened further. "Ah, I see—I am to be denied any information while I convalesce. Then what good am I?"

Videau expelled a long breath. Having finished his quick examination of Henri's wound, he could find no other way to avoid addressing his patient. "The king feels that you have more than earned a rest, and we have no more right to ask more of you. We drove the Catholics back. We cannot fight during the Winter. It will be some time before the French King can raise the money for a force to replace Joyeuse."

Henri could scarcely argue with the surgeon. His victory had virtually made him extraneous for the next few months. With a grimace, he accepted the news. "Very well, I will spend Christmas at home. But by New Year, I will return to La Rochelle."

"If that is God's plan, then it will be so." Like Henri, Videau was a devout follower of Calvin. If God willed a thing, then there was nothing that man nor beast could do to stop it.

❧

The chateau Saint-Jean-d'Angély, typically a sleepy country house, was a hive of activity. Messengers appeared with the shocking news that the Prince de Conde would be unexpectedly returning home, throwing the usual routine of the house into chaos. With less than two days to prepare, the tension was palatable.

Supervising the activity with the precision of a military maneuver, Charlotte Catherine, Princess de Conde oversaw the myriad of duties that needed to be attended to before her husband's return. During Henri's absence, she had proven herself a capable mistress to the staff, despite being barely out of her teens. Her hard-won respect showed in their treatment of his their mistress. "Madame, the cook says that he can serve veal for dinner, but he doubts that he can make the sauce His Highness prefers." Prémilhac de Belcastel approached his mistress, biting his lip. Not much older than his mistress, the page tried in vain to smooth his windblown hair.

"Why can't he make a simple sauce?" Charlotte whirled to face him, her face flushed. As he flinched at her harsh words, her expression softened. "I know it's short notice, but His Highness is injured. I would hope to provide him some comfort while he recovers."

"The Cook says that the herbs he needs only grow in Summer. And it's the herbs that make the sauce so appetizing. Without them, it won't be up to His Highness' expectations."

"We've all been put out of place at his return. Tell the cook that he will have to do whatever he can to make do. I will explain to my husband that we had to modify the sauce."

Belcastel bobbed a quick nod before bounding off to the kitchen. Watching his retreat, Charlotte turned to glance at her list. "We'll simply have to make do. One mustn't grumble when a war hero comes home." If she understood anything, it was the importance of making allowances for a returning soldier. Her grandfather had returned from battles waged across the Italian peninsula with Francis I, a king who rewarded him with the rise in stature and wealth that her family currently enjoyed. Charlotte could do nothing less, given the likelihood that Conde's cousin would inherit the throne from Francis' grandson. If God decided otherwise, there was the family's loyalty to Henri III. Either way, Charlotte's sacrifices the past two years had ensured her security. An interruption during the coldest, most miserable time of the year was a small sacrifice to pay for the security it would win for the future.

She rubbed her eyes with the pad of her thumb. She could make it through the unexpected return of her husband. No matter how ill-tempered he would be when he arrived, she would make sure that the home he returned to would be impeccable.

Henry eyed the men assembled at his bedchamber, narrowing his gaze before emitting a snort. "I see that the Princess has managed to compile quite a staff in my absence. That is to be commended, but perhaps you could tell me just who the devil you all are?'

A stocky, middle-aged man stepped forward and inclined his head. "Highness, I am Michel Brillaud, comptroller of your household."

Henry shot a look at his wife, who blanched under his gaze. "You hired a man to manage my accounts without consulting me?"

"Husband, it was necessary. After the expense of rescuing you from Guernsey, it was necessary to get our accounts in order."

"Expense? You regret your decision to liberate me from that foggy patch of dirt?" His face turned red, and the exertion of sitting up proved to be too much for him. A wince crossed his face, and Charlotte rushed to make him more comfortable.

"No, Highness. No one regrets the expense of getting you safely home from England and Elizabeth's hollow promises. The King of Navarre was determined to get you back to the battlefield, and my lady has no regrets in sending the funds to get you across the Channel. Unfortunately, the war against the Catholic League has proven to be more costly than any of us have expected." Brillaud's words calmed Conde's anger, at least momentarily.

"I take it you now have sufficient funds to run the chateau, Madame." Conde's words ended in a cough, and Charlotte placed a cup of wine into his hands.

"We've done quite well for ourselves, thanks to Brillaud's work." She inclined her blonde head to the elder man, who rewarded her with a modest smile.

"And the others?" Conde returned his attention to the rest of the men assembled in the bedchamber.

"Corbais is my valet, and he will be yours during your stay here." She motioned for the reedy man with a severe cut of brown hair perched upon his head to step forward. "And your cousin Navarre sent Belcastle from Gascony to be my page. Navarre was insistent that we find him an apprenticeship, but I think he has served me well as a page."

Belcastle cleared his throat loudly. "I serve at your pleasure, Highness. It is my honor to do so. And I would gladly serve you during your stay as well." The contrast between the two men was sharp, Belcastle's youthful face the kind of rugged handsomeness that any woman would find attractive. Conde, on the other hand, sported a sharp nose accompanied by an angular face that could only be described as "distinct."

Conde waved his hand, "No, stay in my wife's employ. I have pages enough. Now that I am convalescing, they have little to do but sword fight in the courtyard." He turned to look at Charlotte. "Something bothers you, Madame."

"I fear that we're taxing you too much. We should let you rest."

"My wife is right; I need rest more than anything. Well, more than anything other than to return to battle. Leave me."

Get it for FREE here.

WHO'S WHO AT THE FRENCH COURT

<u>The Royal Family</u>

Catherine de Medici, Queen Mother of France, wife of Henry II.
    Charles, King of France, Catherine's son
    Elizabeth of Austria, Charle's wife
    Henri, Duke of Anjou, Catherine's son
    Louise of Lorraine, Henri's wife
    Francis/ Hercules, Duke of Alençon, Catherine's youngest son
    Margot of Valois, Catherine's daughter

<u>The Bourbons</u>

Jeanne, Queen of Navarre, first cousin of Henry II, due to France's Salic Law, she cannot inherit the French throne, yet her descent through a male relative means any of her male decedents can.
    Antoine, King of Navarre. Jeanne's husband
    Henry, King of Navarre, Jeanne's only surviving son and heir
    Catherine of Bourbon, Henry's only sister
    Henri, Prince of Conde, Henry's first cousin

Marie of Cleves, Henri the Prince of Conde's first cousin and his wife

Henriette of Cleves, Duchess of Nevers, the eldest of the Cleves sisters and close friend of Princess Margot of Valois.

Louis Gonzaga, Duke of Nevers, an Italian who became a naturalized French due to his association with Catherine de Medici. He inherited the title Duke of Nevers from his father-in-law.

The Guise

[Descended from Claude, a younger brother of the Duc de Lorraine, the family retains the epithet "of Lorraine," and strong ties to their Lorraine cousins.]

Anna, Duchess of Guise and Nemours, a granddaughter of Louis XII.
    Francis, her deceased first husband and the second Duke of Guise
    Mary of Guise, Francis's sister and mother of Mary, Queen of Scots
    Henri, Duke of Guise, Anna's eldest son and heir to Guise dukedom
    Catherine of Cleves, Henri's wife and older sister of Marie of Cleves. Became Princess de Porcelian through her first marriage.
    Catherine of Lorraine, Duchess of Montpensier Anna's only daughter
    Louis II, Cardinal of Guise, younger brother of Henri
    Duke of Mayenne, brother of Henri

The Court

Simon, Baron de Sauve, Catherine de Medici's secretary who rose to become one of Charles IX's Secretaries of State.

Charlotte, Baronesse de Sauve and later Marquis of Noirmourtier, his wife.

Compared to her sister, Henriette, Catherine of Cleves, Duchesse de Guise, left a legacy of portraits. The first hangs in the Guise Chateau d'Eu, which I could not resist sending her to in Fate's Mistress.

The second image is credited to Francois Clouet.

The third I can't find a credit for, but it looks like a Clouet portrait, or one by a follower of Clouet.

I was really excited to write Catherine's story because out of the three Cleves sisters, she is easily my favorite. I originally planned to have her and Henri arguing constantly, until I looked at her genealogical chart. I found that she was pregnant for most of the time covered in the book, and there was not evidence whatsoever that any of her children were not the legitimate children of the Duc de Guise.

Did Catherine hire the man who assassinated Henri III? I could not find any evidence that she did or did not. Most contemporaries and historians credit her fiery sister- in-law for the deed. I decided to put forth an alternative theory because Catherine never struck me as a passive woman.

I'll return to Catherine and her daughter, Louise Marguerite, in my novel *The Uncrowned Queen*, which is the story of Gabrielle d'Estrees. Although Louise is credited for being a close friend of Gabrielle during her reign as mistress to Henry IV and the author of a scandalous account of Henry's reign, the math just doesn't work out. Louise was less than ten years old when Gabrielle ruled the French court. It's likely that her "account" is full of stories she heard thirdhand. In order to keep from tearing my hair out with the age problem, Catherine will become one of Gabrielle's confidantes at Henry's court.

Writing this series has been a labor of love. I hope you have enjoyed reading it, and I hope it spurs you to learn more about the women of 16th Century France.

Laura du Pre

ABOUT THE AUTHOR

Laura du Pre is an emerging author of historical fiction. Fate's Mistress is Laura's third book and the third in the Three Graces Trilogy.

Laura holds a Master's Degree in History from Middle Tennessee State University. Before writing full time she worked as an archivist and a contributor for historical publications. She continues to live in the Deep South with her cranky elderly cat, Owen.

You can download a FREE copy of the Three Graces short story *Safe in my Arms* at her website.

Connect with Laura
www.lauradupre.com
laura@lauradupre.com

FURTHER READING ABOUT THE FRENCH RENAISSANCE

I'm indebted to the historians and biographers who came before me.

- Borthwick, Robert Brown. *History of the Princes de Conde in the 16th and 17th Centuries.* Vol I &II, 1872.
- Carroll, Stewart. *Martyrs and Murderers: The Guise Family and the Making of Europe.* 2009.
- Goldstone, Nancy. *Rival Queens: The Rival Queens: Catherine de Medici, Her Daughter Marguerite de Valois, and the Betrayal That Ignited a Kingdom.* 2015
- Knecht, Robert J. *The French Renaissance Court,* 2008.
- —— *The Rise and Fall of Renaissance France,* 1483-1610, 2001.
- Freer, Martha Walker. *Henri III King of France and Poland.* Vol I-III. 1888.
- Marsh, Ann. *History of the Protestant Reformation in France.* 1851.
- Strange, Mark. *Women of Power: The Life and Times of Catherine de Medici.* 1976.
- Williams, H. Noel. *The Brood of False Lorraine: The History of the Ducs de Guise.* Volumes I & II.

www.ingramcontent.com/pod-product-compliance
Lightning Source LLC
Chambersburg PA
CBHW032036180726
48284CB00008B/2609